"It looks like a fairy tale."

Emma smiled up into Brice's eyes. "It's positively enchanting. Even the hardest of hearts would be moved by this kind of beauty."

Brice looked down at her in the darkness and realized his hard heart was moved, but not by the lights or the garden or the star-filled sky. Their movements slowed until finally they were standing still, locked in each other's arms, gazing into each other's eyes. He wanted to kiss her. He was fairly certain she wanted the same thing.

He looked at her. "I'd never want to hurt you, Emma."

"Hurt me? What do you mean?"

After a moment, Brice shook his head. "I only meant that I would never try and take advantage of your trust. Remember that. No matter what happens."

ROMANCE

Dear Reader,

The end of the century is near, and we're all eagerly anticipating the wonders to come. But no matter what happens, I believe that everyone will continue to need and to seek the unquenchable spirit of love…of *romance*. And here at Silhouette Romance, we're delighted to present another month's worth of terrific, emotional stories.

This month, RITA Award-winning author Marie Ferrarella offers a tender BUNDLES OF JOY tale, in which *The Baby Beneath the Mistletoe* brings together a man who's lost his faith and a woman who challenges him to take a chance at love…and family. In Charlotte Maclay's charming new novel, a millionaire playboy isn't sure what he was *Expecting at Christmas,* but what he gets is a *very* pregnant butler! Elizabeth Harbison launches her wonderful new theme-based miniseries, CINDERELLA BRIDES, with the fairy-tale romance—complete with mistaken identity!—between *Emma and the Earl.*

In *A Diamond for Kate* by Moyra Tarling, discover whether a doctor makes his devoted nurse his devoted wife *after* learning about her past.… Patricia Thayer's cross-line miniseries WITH THESE RINGS returns to Romance and poses the question: Can *The Man, the Ring, the Wedding* end a fifty-year-old curse? You'll have to read this dramatic story to find out! And though *The Millionaire's Proposition* involves making a baby in Natalie Patrick's upbeat Romance, can a down-on-her-luck waitress also convince him to make beautiful memories…as man and wife?

Enjoy this month's offerings, and look forward to a new century of timeless, traditional tales guaranteed to touch your heart!

Mary-Theresa Hussey

Mary-Theresa Hussey
Senior Editor, Silhouette Romance

Please address questions and book requests to:
Silhouette Reader Service
U.S.: 3010 Walden Ave., P.O. Box 1325, Buffalo, NY 14269
Canadian: P.O. Box 609, Fort Erie, Ont. L2A 5X3

EMMA
AND THE EARL

Elizabeth Harbison

Silhouette
R O M A N C E™
Published by Silhouette Books
America's Publisher of Contemporary Romance

To Neville White, my English pen pal of many years, who may well have an intriguing secret identity...

Special thanks to the Silveiras: Helen, for the friendship and tea; and Mark, for saving my computer— and, by extension, my life—time and again. And thanks also to Swoffers Estate Agents, Guernsey.

 SILHOUETTE BOOKS

ISBN 0-373-19410-2

EMMA AND THE EARL

Copyright © 1999 by Elizabeth Harbison

Visit us at www.romance.net

Printed in U.S.A.

ELIZABETH HARBISON

has been an avid reader for as long as she can remember. After devouring the Nancy Drew and Trixie Beldon series in grade school, she moved on to the suspense of Mary Stewart, Dorothy Eden and Daphne du Maurier, just to name a few. From there it was a natural progression to writing, although early efforts have been securely hidden away in the back of a closet.

After authoring three cookbooks, Elizabeth turned her hand to writing romances and hasn't looked back. Her second book for Silhouette Romance, *Wife Without a Past*, was a 1998 finalist for the Romance Writers of America's prestigious RITA Award in the "Best Traditional Romance" category.

Elizabeth lives in Maryland with her husband, John, and daughter, Mary Paige, as well as two dogs, Bailey and Zuzu. She loves to hear from readers and you can write to her at c/o Box 1636, Germantown, MD 20875.

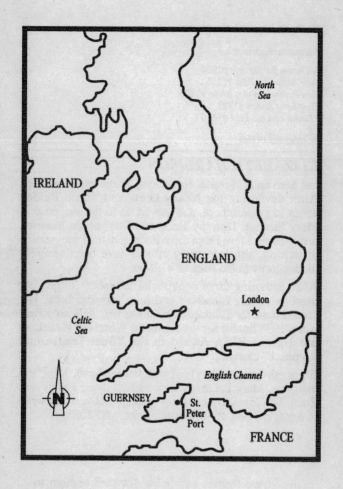

Prologue

June 9, 1998

3431 41st St., N.W.
Apartment #202
Washington, D.C. 20017
U.S.A.

The Right Hon. Brice, The Earl of Palliser
Sheldale House
St. Peter Port
Guernsey, Channel Islands GY1 2NU
U.K.

Dear Sir:

  Please forgive my being forward enough to write to you at your residence. I am a pharmaceutical horticulturist with NBL Botanical Laboratory in Washington, D.C., and will be in

England between July 5-12.

After seeing your estate in John Turnhill's photography book of English country gardens, I have reason to believe there is a very rare medicinal plant on the grounds of Sheldale House. If there is any way possible that I could tour the gardens during my trip, I would be most grateful. While I realize this is an unusual request, I feel it would be invaluable to my work at NBL.

I apologize for not giving you more notice, but I've only just made plans to visit your country. Please send word to me either at the above address or, in July, at the Sunnington Hotel, Hampstead, London.

Sincerely,
Emma Lawrence

June 9, 1998

3431 41st St., N.W.
Apartment #202
Washington, D.C. 20017
U.S.A.

18 Cecile Park Road
Crouch End
London, N8 9AS
U.K.

Dear John,

Forgive the kitschy Washington, D.C., postcard, but I wanted to get this note off to you as soon as possible, so I had to settle for what the lunch joint across the street from work had to offer. It was this or that hideous letterhead at work. By the way, when I tried to look up your phone number, the international operator said you were unlisted!

So anyway, are you ready for the big news? (Drum roll here, please): we're *finally* going to meet!

The lab is sending me to the U.K. from July 5-12. There's a symposium on the sixth and seventh that I have to attend, but after that, apart from a few things I have to try and arrange, my schedule is going to be really flexible. Hope yours will be too…? I'm dying to see what you look like (why didn't you ever send a picture?!) I know this isn't much notice, but that's the way it always seems to go around here, as you know all too well.

If you don't get this in time to write me at home, you can contact me at a hotel called the Sunnington in Hampstead as of the fifth.

I'm out of room! Gotta run!

　　　　　　　　　　　　love,
　　　　　　　　　　　　Emma

Chapter One

"Let me get this straight. This American gardener to whom you've been writing love notes for two years *in my name* is finally coming to London and wants to meet you?"

Robert Brice Sorrelsby Palliser, the seventeenth earl of Palliser, looked at his friend, John Turnhill, in the mirror behind him. "She's a *pharmaceutical horticulturist,* and I would hardly characterize our letters as "love notes." But other than that, you've got it right, yes."

John smiled, a little smugly. "And you want my permission to continue the charade and impersonate me in the flesh?"

Brice gave a resigned nod. "I can't see any other way around it."

John shook his head, clearly relishing Brice's dilemma. "I cannot believe it. Is this the same Brice

Palliser who sold the most successful daily newspaper in Britain because he felt that kind of journalism was 'dishonest'?''

"It *is* dishonest."

John gave a shout of laughter. "So is pretending to be someone you're not."

Brice started a hot objection, then paused. John was right. For two years Brice had corresponded with Emma Lawrence using John's name and address in London, only a few miles away from Brice's own London home. Regardless of his reasons—reasons which were very good and completely understandable—when you came right down to it, it was a deception.

Two years ago, John had published a photography book of English country gardens, and Emma, spotting an unusual flower in a photo of Brice's Sheldale House garden, on Guernsey in the Channel Islands, had written to John asking about it. Since Brice was more familiar with the plant than John was, John passed the letter on to him. Brice, in turn, had answered for John. At the time it had seemed a good, efficient way to answer Emma's query.

Brice's correspondence with Emma had been very impersonal, at first. But then she'd written again, and something in her response had moved him. "I couldn't help but laugh when you mentioned you were off to microwave a 'pitiful chicken dinner,'" she'd written. "Believe it or not, I had the same thing on the table in front of me. I'm starting to think we're cut from the same cloth. If you told me it was overcooked and rubbery, despite your best efforts, I'd be sure...." He'd written back, not wanting to break the illusion he'd created, both for Emma and for himself. Before he knew it, a close friendship had developed. By then it was too late to tell her he wasn't who she thought he was.

"How do you decide when it's okay to lie and when it's not?" John asked Brice now, his freckled face twitching into a goading grin.

"This was not a typical lie," Brice said calmly. "The difference is in the intent. I didn't tell Emma I was John Turnhill for any malicious reason, or to take advantage of her. You know as well as I do that I wrote that letter for you in your name as a favor because you were in a pinch. I never dreamed it would lead to any sort of personal correspondence."

"Come on, old man." John thumped his friend on the shoulder. "You've had a couple of years to tell her the truth now. Why haven't you?"

"It's ironic, I'll concede that." Brice bit out the words. The truth even sounded like a lie to his own ears. "But the reason is that she has a...a *thing*, as she puts it, about honesty."

"A *thing*?"

"It's really important to her. And rightly so." He wouldn't say more. It had been a confidence Emma had shared with him. He wasn't going to give John the details, no matter how much they might support his own case. "The fact of the matter is that by the time I *should* have told her the truth, it was already too late."

"It's never too late to tell a woman you're the earl of Palliser." John gave a cynical laugh and gestured around the ornate room. "Surely she'd be thrilled to find out your true identity, rather than believe you're plain old me."

Brice looked at him seriously. "No, she wouldn't."

John studied Brice for a moment, then sat down in the Louis XVI chair in the light of a high narrow window. "Even if that's so, I honestly don't see how you can pull this off. A lot of people in this country know who you are on sight, especially women who read articles titled 'The Ten Most Eligible Bachelors in Europe.' How are you planning to avoid that kind of recognition?"

Brice gave a heavy sigh. John was right, he had gotten some of that kind of publicity over the years. Every now and then he learned of another magazine or newspaper who had put him on a bachelor list. "Emma wouldn't read that kind of article."

"But what if she did?"

Brice shrugged, certain she hadn't. "How many people would really recognize me in the flesh after just seeing one or two badly reproduced photos?"

"That's the question. If you ask me, you're recognizable even from a bad photo."

Brice looked at his reflection in a gilded mirror on the wall. His dark hair, slightly wavy and a little longer than usual, was fairly ordinary. On the other hand, his distinct Palliser bone structure—the high cheekbones and straight brow—were easily distinguished. The green eyes, which everyone likened to his late father's, seemed somehow conspicuous.

"Look," John said, interrupting his thoughts.

"Why don't you just tell her the truth and let the proverbial chips fall where they may? It seems a lot easier than all this agonizing."

"I don't want to lose her," Brice heard himself say, and realized that it was true. It might be selfish, but he wanted to preserve his friendship with Emma at any cost. "This is the only relationship that I've ever had with someone who accepts me for myself alone and not for this…" he gestured around the room, "this persona."

"In leaving out this persona," John gestured as Brice had done, "haven't you left out a great deal of who you really are?"

Brice followed the sweep of John's arm, assessing the office of his London home. Oriental carpets covered a gleaming wood floor. The high walls were adorned with priceless art and tapestries. His eye fell on a Remington painting, whose value was higher than that of some people's homes. This wasn't exactly the impression he had given Emma of his life, he knew. "Maybe."

John gave a knowing nod. "And you've used my name to do it. That's two enormous lies right there. It's a tangled web all right."

Unbelievably tangled, Brice thought with an inner groan. Almost schizophrenic. Yet for everything he'd left out in telling her about himself, he'd revealed something more important, in many ways more true. That was at the core of his dilemma, in fact: one of the main reasons Brice was reluctant to tell Emma who he really was, was that in his letters he'd been free to be the man he really wanted to be but couldn't. He'd been light, fanciful at times, even funny. He'd never gone into the subject of his duties, his public persona, the historical estates he had to maintain, the international company he had to run. The heavy weight of his responsibilities lifted every time he picked up the pen as John.

Emma would be hugely disappointed to learn that the man she'd been writing to all this time was a serious, duty-minded aristocrat, who might have dreamed of dancing in the fountain in front of the Ritz on paper, but who would never even consider such a thing in his real life.

When John spoke again, he was very serious. "You have to be very careful about getting involved with someone, remember."

"I know."

"Unless you're ready to tell your mother the truth about Caroline...."

Caroline Fortescue was the daughter of Brice's father's business partner. Though both men had passed away several years back, there was an expectation among remaining family members, most notably Brice's mother, that Brice and Caroline would marry.

It made sense as a business merger: the budding Fortescue microchip technology together with the Palliser telecommunications technology would dominate the market. Their parents thought it was "a good match," and they'd been heavy-handed in their persuasion ever since Caroline and Brice had been in their early twenties. Finally, for the sake of living in peace with their parents, the two had decided to pretend to agree with the plan until they'd found what they really wanted. They were very sure of one thing though, they would never marry each other.

Brice groaned. "If I tell my mother that Caroline and I have no real intentions of getting married, she'll go on a matchmaking campaign the likes of which would have made Wellington quake with fear." He shook his head. "I'm not up for that just yet."

Brice's parents had made "a good match," and as a result Brice had grown up with cold, distant parents who had more regard for appearances than they did for each other. Now his mother was fully willing to extend that legacy to him. Living alone, he'd found out at age twenty, was a far warmer experience than living with two people who led such pointedly separate lives. Perhaps when two people loved, living together was something different than he had experienced. But unconditional love was for other people. He'd never experience it—how could he? His very name created conditions that would be difficult to live with, not the least of which was the occasional public scrutiny.

"Until you say otherwise, and firmly," John said, "Caroline is a consideration."

"That's right."

"Then you'll have to let this Emma know," John persisted. "Before she gets dreamy ideas about herself and you and inadvertently creates havoc for you both."

That was one worry he didn't have, thank goodness. "Emma has no romantic interest in me whatsoever." Brice reflected on this relief for a moment, watching the silent sway of the trees in a gentle wind, then snapped himself out of it. "So that's not a consideration. She need never know."

John didn't look convinced. "If you're sure...?"

"I'm sure." He spoke with complete confidence. "So what about it? Can I use your house while she's here? You're going to be gone anyway, right?"

"I am, yes."

"Then it will be perfect. I have to get away from here." Brice leaned against the windowsill and looked out. The lawn fanned out a long way to the wrought-iron fence bordering the quiet street in South Kensington. Though it was a sunny warm day, no one was out. No one was ever out.

He couldn't invite Emma here, even if he wanted to. It would be like a big wet towel on her vacation. The neighborhood was austere, full of people like him—people who lived quiet, shadowed lives. He wondered if anyone had ever really had *fun* here. Was it even possible? He doubted it. He *had* to use John's home for Emma's visit, just in case she insisted on seeing where he lived. "You know I wouldn't ask if I didn't think it was absolutely necessary."

"I know." John looked at him in silence for a moment, then smiled. "All right. If you insist on going through with this, I don't see how I can protect you from yourself." He reached into his pocket and pulled out a ring of three keys. He dropped them onto the end table with a clang. "Now that I think of it, perhaps this is just what you need to get out of your slump."

Brice looked at him sharply. "What slump?"

John gave him a patient look. "The one that's made you the most grim, serious man in the country. The one that you've been in for the last—how old are you?"

"You're exaggerating. I'm not that bad."

"No? The *Independent* recently referred to you as a living heart donor."

Brice grimaced. "That's a very old joke. I would have thought they could do better than that." He didn't want to reflect on any nugget of truth behind the statement.

John shrugged. "You've got to admit, you haven't been the most jubilant fellow in the world. Maybe this will lighten you up some. Now, about the house. Sarah's leaving for Venice on the second of July. I'll be following by a day. After that, the place is yours."

"Excellent."

They were interrupted by a discreet knock at the door. A maid entered holding a silver tray with a special delivery letter on it. She extended this to Brice, who took it from the tray and nodded a dismissal.

Brice glanced at the envelope and felt a sense of dread. He tore open the letter, read it, and felt the blood leave his face. "Good God."

"What is it?"

"Trouble. This just came from Sheldale House on Guernsey." Brice shook his head and held the letter out to John.

"'Dear Sir,'" John read aloud. "Blah, blah, blah, 'will be in England between July fifth and twelfth. If there is any way possible that I could tour the gardens on my trip,' blah, blah, blah, 'send word at' blah blah blah…'' He looked at Brice and raised his eyebrows. ''So?''

''Look at the signature.''

John looked. ''Emma Lawrence,'' he read, then his mouth dropped open. ''This?'' He pointed at the letter. ''Same woman?''

Brice nodded. ''She must have sent it there the same day she wrote to me here in London.'' He took the paper from John and wadded it into a ball. It had been years since their correspondence had anything to do with the gardens at Sheldale. It hadn't even occurred to him that she might still be interested in seeing them.

''So what's the big problem?'' John asked.

''The problem is that she can't go near the place without discovering who I am.''

''You could have the staff take down all the portraits and photos,'' John suggested.

''And ask them to pretend I'm someone else, that they don't recognize me?'' Brice scoffed. ''Be serious.''

''It's not as though you have to go with her, you know. Send her along to look the place over and see her when she gets back.''

''And run the risk of her seeing something or hearing something that will give me away and I won't even know it?'' The possibilities made his mind reel. ''I can't take that chance.''

A long silence hung between them.

''What are you going to do?'' John asked at last.

"I'm not going to answer." Brice expelled a long breath. Not answering went against every fiber of his responsible being. "It's the only thing I can do. The earl is out of commission for the time being."

"Until she sees you," John pointed out. "Obviously she's a bit more familiar with 'the earl' than you thought. She managed to find your address."

"Any resourceful person could have done that," Brice said. "It doesn't mean she knows what I look like. She probably thinks I'm a doddering old man."

"What about when she gets here? With Palliser Telecommunications going public, your picture has been in the newspaper several times this week already."

He knew. "That's local news," he said, more to himself than to John. "They wouldn't know about that in America. At any rate, I'm quite sure she won't be reading the financial pages while she's here."

Emma stumbled out of customs at Heathrow Airport, thanks to slick new shoes and a polished linoleum floor, and almost fell right into the newsagent's kiosk, knocking one of the papers to the floor in several pieces. "I'm sorry," she said, stooping to gather them together again. A headline caught her eye: Palliser Telecommunications Prices Skyrocket as Economy Rises. Palliser! The very man she wanted to see. She picked that section of the paper up to look closer.

"You going to pay for that?" the seller asked sharply, startling her.

"Oh. Yes, of course." She started to reach for her purse, then remembered that she hadn't changed any of her money yet. "Sorry, I don't have any cash…" Under the man's dark scrutiny, she reassembled the newspaper and handed it back to him. "Jeez, welcome to England," she said, under her breath.

She walked away, wishing she could have seen a picture of the earl of Palliser. He hadn't answered her letter before she left and she was getting nervous. She hoped he was a kindly old man who would be glad to let her tour the gardens of his estate, but as time wore on she pictured him more and more as a pointy, mean, middle-aged dandy, who had tossed her letter in the trash as soon as he'd gotten it, cursing her American brashness for even asking.

Maybe he'd even gotten on John's case about it, since she had mentioned his book in her letter. Perhaps that was why John was so vague every time she asked him anything about the earl or Sheldale House in her letters. She hoped not. It hadn't occurred to her that if the earl didn't like personal contact, he might blame John for it.

No, that was borrowing trouble. John would have said something if the earl had given him a hard time. He didn't hold things back from her. She smiled at the thought of finally meeting him, then immediately felt a twinge of nerves. The unwelcome thought that he might be disappointed when he saw her flew to mind. There was no telling how he pictured her in his mind, but she worried that he'd expect some tall, thin, blond California-type beauty. If so, he was in for a surprise.

Emma was plain. She had ordinary facial features, nondescript brown eyes, a plain old straight nose, an ordinary smile. At five feet eight inches, she was tall but not willowy or especially thin, or any of the things that made being tall a desirable trait for a woman.

Usually she went about her life and her work without thinking much about her appearance. Normally it didn't matter. And it shouldn't matter now, she realized. She and John were already great friends, it wasn't as though either one of them expected it to lead to anything more.

Attraction wasn't an issue.

She wondered, ruefully, if it was the habit of all women or just those who were particularly insecure about their looks to feel like it always was an issue. There hadn't been a job interview, a party, or a blind date where Emma hadn't felt the same self-consciousness.

This was what was good about her relationship with John. They liked each other for who they truly *were*, not for their looks, their jobs, their finances, or anything else that could be summarized in a demographic label.

It was the most...what was the word? *Honest* came to mind. It was the most honest relationship she'd ever had.

The two-day symposium on holistic medicine in the twenty-first century seemed to Emma to last two years, partly because of her jet lag and partly because of her eagerness to get it over with and meet John. After the first day, she'd been disappointed to return to the hotel and find no message from him. She couldn't call him because she didn't have the number, despite the fact that she had again tried the information operator and the phone book. She hadn't heard from him since sending the card about her visit, so she wasn't even positive he knew she was in London.

During the second day of the symposium, she could barely follow the debate about the medical use of marijuana because she was trying to decide what to do if there was still no message from John when she got back. She had his address. If worse came to worst, she could always just show up and knock on his door, but she really didn't want to do that. Emma was not a fan of surprises, either giving them or receiving them.

When the group finally let out on the second day, she was so eager to get back to the hotel that she took a cab rather than saving the money and figuring out the bus schedule. The desk clerk called to her as soon as she walked in the door.

"Message for you, miss," he said, with a knowing smile. Emma had asked him about messages at least twice a day since she'd arrived. He looked at her over the wire rims of his glasses, and handed her a folded yellow slip of paper.

She could barely breathe as she opened it. "John Turnhill rang," it said, "at 4:10 p.m. Would like to take you to dinner. Can you make it tonight?" He had also left a phone number. At last!

She turned to ask the clerk if she could use the phone, but before she could speak, he nudged it toward her. "Dial direct," he said, then deliberately turned to busy himself with the mail slots in order to give Emma some privacy.

With a shaking hand she dialed the number on the paper. When he answered, she went weak at the sound of his voice. She tried to speak, but all that came out was an embarrassing squeak. She cleared her throat and tried again. "John? This is Emma," she said.

"Emma." Was it her imagination or was there tension in his voice? "I'm so glad to hear from you."

She breathed a sigh of relief. She must have imagined the tension. She swallowed. "I got your message. Dinner tonight sounds great. What time?"

"How about if I pick you up at half past seven?"

She looked at her watch. Half past. That meant 7:30, which meant she'd have two hours to get ready. "Perfect," she said. Her entire body was tingling with anticipation. "Do you know how to get here?"

"Yes, I can manage."

She didn't want to let him hang up. She'd waited so long for this that she was half afraid it was a dream that would pop like a bubble if she wasn't very careful.

"So I'll see you then," he said, again sounding a little stiff.

"Great," she said quickly. *Don't sound over-eager,* she told herself. "Until then."

When she hung up the phone she noticed that her hand was shaking like a dry leaf in the wind. *Breathe, Emma. You've got two hours to calm down.*

"Boyfriend?" the desk clerk asked, taking the phone back.

"Nope. Just an old friend." She felt her face grow warm. "A pen pal, actually. We've never met before."

"Ah." He nodded, and gave her a commiserative smile. "You look nervous."

"I'm more nervous than I've ever been in my life." The words came out in a rush.

"You needn't be, a lovely girl like yourself." He gave a quick smile and said very seriously, "Your friend will be very happy when he sees you, I'm certain."

Chapter Two

Emma went back to her room, buoyed by the desk clerk's compliment. Yes, perhaps he was just being nice. It was his job, after all. But he had such an honest face that she allowed herself to believe him. *A lovely girl like yourself. Your friend will be very happy when he sees you, I'm certain.*

She returned her thoughts to work and sat down on the bed to take her notebook out of her bag. As she leafed through her notes from the day, she realized that she'd been so distracted that she hadn't even written complete sentences. She'd been more consumed with anticipation than she'd realized. Now she'd have to rewrite all the notes before she forgot what they meant. With a sigh, she looked at her watch and hoped she'd have at least a little time after she'd finished to get ready for dinner.

The task took a little more than an hour, and when

she was finished her hand was aching, but her purpose in coming had been reinforced. Part of her had been so eager to meet John that she'd let the goal of going to the earl of Palliser's estate slip to the back burner. Now she remembered just how important it was.

When she'd first seen John's photo of the earl's Sheldale House garden on Guernsey, she'd been so surprised she nearly spilled her hot coffee in her lap. For nearly three years she and her boss had been researching natural alternative painkillers for arthritis and had narrowed it down to Schilus mucre, or St. Paul's Heart, a very rare plant related to Barren Wort, which was itself a rare English plant.

Yet there, plain as the grass in John's picture, was what looked like a large patch of St. Paul's Heart. They'd examined the photo closely and determined that it looked very similar. Then funding for the research had run low and they'd been forced to turn their priorities elsewhere. Until a month ago, that was, when a new benefactor had donated nearly one million dollars to them for medical research. Emma had volunteered to come to the symposium and stay on using her vacation time in hopes of researching the plants and conditions at Sheldale House.

It was a goal she shouldn't lose sight of, no matter how excited she was about meeting John. In fact, she might even need John to help her with it. Much as she hated to do it, if she didn't hear from the earl soon—like on her way out the door this evening— she was going to have to ask John if he could pull any strings to get her permission to visit Sheldale

House. Heaven knew she didn't want to do it. After their initial correspondence, she'd tried to keep business out of their relationship, but if she explained to him how important it was, maybe he would want to help. That thought boosted her optimism considerably.

She set her notes aside and went to the cupboard for a towel so she could get showered and ready for dinner. She bathed quickly and dried her hair. After trying three different ''meeting John'' outfits, she finally settled on a simple yellow sundress, cut in a classic forties' style that created the illusion of a narrow waist thanks to a full skirt. It wasn't one of her new ''going to London'' outfits, but it was an old favorite that she felt comfortable in.

Her hair, as usual, was proving to be a problem. It fell halfway down her back in a thick tangle of auburn curls. After trying several possibilities, she finally decided to let it hang in wild curls about her shoulders. Luckily all the latest fashion magazines were heralding that look as ''pre-Raphaelite fabulous,'' which she supposed was a good thing. She brushed some color on her cheeks and lips, the way the girl at the drugstore had taught her, and went downstairs to wait for John.

She went to the front step and sat in the balmy evening air, drinking in the sights, sounds and smells of London. The sky was deepening blue, with streaks of lipstick pink stretching across the horizon. Some of the birds in the leafy green trees were singing new songs, unfamiliar to Emma.

A small blue car pulled up outside the hotel. That,

Emma realized as she looked at its tiny dimensions, must be what they call a Mini. There was a man in it, alone. Her heart tripped. It was almost certainly John. The time had finally come.

The man got out of the car and walked toward the hotel. He was tall, with a lean, muscular build. His dark hair, just a bit longish at the collar, gleamed in the amber evening sunlight, bringing Sir Lancelot to mind.

But nothing could have prepared her for the exquisite dignity of his face or, more specifically, her heart-pounding reaction to it. Even from a distance, she was struck by the masculine square jaw, and the sensual perfection of his curved mouth. His cheekbones were strong and noble-looking without being so high as to be "pretty." As he drew closer, she could see that his straight dark brows framed pale, intelligent eyes. Eyes that made her feel, for one irrational moment, that she was home.

"Hello," he said, nearing her.

"Hi," she said, but it sounded like a question. Was it him? Was it really him?

He stopped before her and cocked his head slightly to the side. "Emma?"

She gave a slight nod—the best she could do, considering the fact that his looks had practically paralyzed her—and only then realized that she'd been holding her breath.

He smiled, extending his hand. "I'm John Turnhill."

It *was* him. Had she ever even imagined he would be so handsome? That old familiar self-consciousness about her own looks resurfaced. "I'm very pleased to meet you," she said, holding out her hand.

He held her gaze easily as he took her hand in his. "You are exactly as I imagined."

Something about the way he said it put her at ease. She believed him, and it was okay. "Am I?"

"Exactly." He let go of her hand and they started to walk side-by-side to the car. "So how do you like London so far, Emma?"

"I really love it," she said, hoping he couldn't hear her thundering heart. It had to be nerves, she told herself. After all, this was *John*. She knew him already, there was nothing to be nervous about.

"Good. I've chosen a little place for dinner just around the corner in Hampstead Heath." His voice was low and rich, with a perfectly measured English accent. That part of it was as she'd imagined. "I hope you like French food?"

He had once mentioned in his letters wanting to take her to the famous Thames Gate Restaurant. Had he changed his mind? She had the unwelcome thought that perhaps he was embarrassed to be seen with her since she wasn't beautiful. But he wasn't like that, she knew he wasn't. It was probably just because he was on a budget, like she was. It was all well and good to *say* you wanted to take someone to a fancy restaurant, but it wasn't so easily done. "Yes, I love French food," she said. "That sounds great."

"I realize it's not typically British, but the food is quite good, and it's in one of London's most Dickensian spots. I thought you'd prefer that to boiled potatoes in the business district."

She laughed. "You made the right call."

He led her to the Mini and opened the door for her. She smiled and, as gracefully as possible, folded her five-foot-eight-inch frame into the car. John had to be at least six feet tall, probably taller. The Mini seemed like an odd choice of car for him, though he had less trouble getting in gracefully than she had.

Driving it was another story. After he ground the gear into first and lurched the car out into the street, they drove in silence for a couple of miles before John said, "I have to admit, this is a bit awkward for me."

"It *is* a funny little car," she agreed, wondering why the car struck her as so discordant with the man.

He gave a brief laugh. "No—well, yes, but I meant meeting this way. After all this time."

"Oh, *that*. Me, too." She glanced at him, but her self-consciousness surged again, and she decided it was best to concentrate on the passing scenery so she could actually get a few sentences out without being dazzled by his looks. "You know, suddenly I feel like we don't really know each other at all." She glanced back at him.

He gave a sober nod. "I think it's safe to say there are a lot of things we don't know about each other." He glanced over at her as he drew to a halt at a pedestrian crossing. "Quite a lot."

A tremor buzzed through her. Excitement? Or trepidation? She couldn't say. "Sounds like someone's got some skeletons in the closet. Or the tower."

"The tower?" He glanced at her, then put the car back into gear and edged forward.

"You know, the Tower of London." She laughed nervously, immediately embarrassed at the lame joke and wishing she could take it back. "Sorry, I've had the aristocracy on my mind for the past few days." That didn't come out right either. "I mean, it's impossible not to in a city like this. It can really make an ordinary person feel like a peasant."

"Ah." He watched the road in front of him, but she noticed his grip adjust and tighten on the steering wheel. "Well, chimney sweep or...or earl, isn't it what's inside that counts?"

She breathed a sigh of relief. He was picking it up instead of just letting her comment fall with a thud. "I've always thought it only mattered what was on the inside." She looked at his handsome profile and smiled to herself. Nothing wrong with that outside though, she thought. "As long as you're honest about it."

He stiffened and kept his eyes fastened on the road. "Right." He turned the car into a sleepy Georgian block just north of Hampstead Heath. The street was lined with tall trees, and narrow alleys with tiny shops: booksellers, herbalists, boutiques. Several pubs that they passed had tables set up outside. "Although sometimes people have very good reasons for not telling the truth."

She wrinkled her nose. "I don't know that there's ever a good reason to lie to someone you care about and trust." She didn't elaborate. She didn't need to. Several months ago, she'd finally told John about an incident which had nearly destroyed her career and had wreaked havoc with her emotions.

Eight years back, when she'd been working at a pharmaceutical laboratory, her supervisor had helped himself to the inventory after hours using a magnetized identification card that was linked to Emma, just in case he got caught. He'd been careful to use the duplicate card only late at night, when Emma wasn't likely to come in with her original card. He'd viewed her as a plain Jane, correctly guessing that she would have little or no social life, and thus no alibi for her late-night hours. She'd been the perfect person to frame. Indeed, when the crime was detected, Emma had been under heavy scrutiny for the first several weeks of the investigation.

When all was said and done, the worst part of it for Emma was knowing that her supervisor had been stealing for months and lying to her all that time. She would never have dreamed he was betraying her that way.

"I know you feel strongly about telling the truth," John said, parking in front of a charming restaurant called *La Fontaine du Mars*. He got out of the car and came around to open Emma's door for her. It was a small gallantry, but still appreciated. "I do, too, really. I only meant that sometimes people lie with good intentions." He took a bracing breath. "Anyway, this is a nice little place to eat. Usually they have tables set out in the morning and people come for coffee and to watch the world go by. It's a good place for that."

"I can imagine."

They walked toward the ivy-clad front door. Emma thought of the help she needed from John in getting to Brice Palliser and wondered if he would find it dishonest of her to ask for that kind of help. "It is all in the intention," she agreed, deciding it would be best for her to mention the favor before they ate, rather than running the risk of appearing to butter him up first.

The restaurant was as charming inside as out. The walls were made of weathered brick, and a huge fireplace sat dormant at one end of the room. The red-checked tablecloths were worn but clean, and the unlit candles on each table were secured in various old, mostly inexpensive, wine bottles. It was quietly intimate, and she was suddenly glad he hadn't chosen a more famous and probably austere place instead. This was comfortable and comfort was definitely helpful right now.

"John," she said, after they were seated and had studied their menus for a few minutes.

He didn't answer.

"John," she said again, louder.

There was another moment's hesitation before he made a small exclamation and said, "Sorry. Did you say something to me?"

"Yes." She gathered her nerve. She really hated to ask this of him, but she had to, and she had to do it now and get it over with. "I'm afraid I have a favor to ask of you. A big favor, that is." She sucked air in through her teeth. "A really big favor."

"Of course. What is it?"

Three solid heartbeats passed. "I need to meet Brice Palliser."

Was it her imagination or did his face pale? "Why do you need to meet *him?*"

He sounded stung. "Actually, I don't really need to meet him," she said quickly. "I just need to talk with him. Specifically, I need permission to go to his estate and dig around in the gardens a little."

"Sheldale House." His voice was monotone.

"That's right."

The restaurant lights dimmed and the waitress came to the table to light the candle. "Would you like some wine with dinner?" she asked.

"Please. Could you bring a bottle of Dom—" He stopped, cleared his throat. "How about a sparkling wine of some sort?" He looked to Emma for approval.

"Great." She nodded.

He looked at the menu, and pointed one out. "This is from a good region."

The waitress made a note on her pad, then asked Emma, "Are you ready to order?"

Emma hesitated, unsure of the budget. Though he'd never specifically said, she guessed from his job description that John wasn't much better off than she, so she looked down the right-hand side of the menu for the least expensive dishes. She was about to order the grilled chicken breast when John spoke.

"How about the filet mignon with bearnaise?" he suggested. "The beef is local and quite good."

"Filet mignon? Really?" Emma couldn't even remember the last time she'd had real steak instead of hamburger.

He raised an eyebrow. "Does it not appeal to you?"

"I'd love it, but..." She lowered her voice and spoke through her teeth. "It's kind of pricey..."

"Don't worry about *that*. If it's something you want, you're certainly worth it." He smiled, and his eyes lit a flame in her heart.

"Well, it *does* sound good—"

"Then it's settled." He slapped his menu shut. "The filet for both of us," he said to the waitress, keeping his eyes on Emma.

"Are you sure about this?" Emma asked, when the waitress had gone. She was warmed by the idea that he was trying so hard to make it a memorable evening for her, but worried that he was overextending himself to do it.

"Absolutely," he said, without a trace of doubt. "Now. Where were we?"

"Brice Palliser."

He looked startled for a moment, then his expression relaxed some and he said, "The garden."

She nodded, noting for the second time that he wanted to keep the subject off the man. Clearly there was discomfort there, and she wondered if John thought she'd rather meet the earl than spend time with him. "Right, the garden," she said, trying to reassure him. "Frankly, I'm not sure I have much use for the man. You know, I tried writing to him for permission, but he didn't even bother to respond.

You'd think he could at least have had his secretary or someone write back.''

He looked pained. ''We-ell. Maybe he didn't get your letter. He may be out of the country. He travels quite a lot, you know.''

''But doesn't he have a private secretary?''

''Not at home,'' he said, then added quickly, ''Or, uh, did you write to him at his office?''

''Home, I guess. Sheldale House on Guernsey.''

John clicked his tongue against his teeth. ''I don't think he goes there very often.''

Hope deflated. ''There's no way to get in touch with him at all? For permission, I mean.''

John laced his hands before him on the table and considered for a moment, before he said, ''This is really important to you, I know.'' He let out a pent-up breath and raked a hand through his hair. ''Sorry. I feel bad that I let it go this long. I should have arranged for you to go to Guernsey as soon as I got your letter.''

Emma reached across the table and touched his arm. ''John, this isn't *your* responsibility. There was no reason you should have made the arrangements for me, that's my job.'' She tried to lighten it with a laugh. ''I don't even think I mentioned Sheldale in my letter to you. I'm only asking your help now because it doesn't look like the man is going to bother to answer a nobody like me, at least in his eyes.''

''Emma, it's not like that—''

''Here we go,'' the waitress called, reappearing with their wine. She set the glasses down, then opened the bottle, poured them each a glass, and left with a promise to bring their dinners along in a few minutes.

Emma watched her go, then said, "To be fair, I didn't tell the earl of Palliser just how important this might be. I didn't want to overstate it because if I'm wrong, I'm just a crackpot, you know? I didn't want to make any grand claims that could later be called lies or exaggerations. Especially not to this fancy-schmancy earl, who would probably think I was just trying to rub elbows with the upper crust."

He stiffened. "Why would he think that?"

"Well, I'm *not*, of course," she hastened to amend. "You know that." She took a sip of her wine, then gestured with the glass. "What I meant was, he's rich and powerful. I suspect people are approaching him for money and favors all the time."

"Not like this." When she looked at him, he added, "Probably." He smiled then, snatching her breath away.

She shrugged. "Maybe not, but he doesn't know me from any of the rest of the masses."

His smile faded slightly. "It's definitely a tough situation." There was weight in his words. Emma found herself trying to figure out why. After a pause, he went on, "But I think perhaps you're underestimating him."

"Really?" She was interested. "How well do you know him?"

He frowned, started to speak then stopped. After another moment, he said, "That's hard to say." He poured more wine into her glass. "Well enough to know that he really means well, but doesn't always know how to juggle all of his responsibilities.''

"Does he really have that much to keep track of?''

"You'd be surprised." He finished his wine in a gulp. "A multi-national company, several estates—there's quite a lot, actually.''

"I see." She wanted to believe it, but something told her there was more to it than that. "Then maybe he *didn't* get my letter. Maybe, as you said, he's out of the country." A moment passed. "Then again, he may have got it and ignored it. There's just no way of knowing.''

He appeared to consider that carefully. "If that's the case, then I'm sure he had his reasons.''

Emma felt a twinge of guilt. She was starting to get the feeling that John's friendship with the earl was closer than he'd indicated. She tried to lighten things up with a laugh. "Do you always play devil's advocate?''

He smiled again, and she was relieved that the tension seemed to be broken. "Only when the poor devil isn't able to defend himself. Listen, Emma, let me see what I can do about arranging some time at Sheldale House," he said, then added, more to himself, "Though I don't see how you could stay there.''

"*Stay* there?" Such a thought had never even occurred to her. "No, no, I don't want to stay there, I just want to hunt around the grounds.''

"It's holiday season," he said, taking a sip of his wine. "It won't be easy to find accommodations on Guernsey itself.''

"I'll pitch a tent outside the estate, I don't mind.''

He studied her for a minute, then said, "You're very determined."

Self-conscious, she tilted her head toward the window. "I am where this is concerned." Outside, the sun was dipping behind the buildings into dusk, providing little light to compete with the candles in the small bistro. It was intoxicating.

"Determination is an admirable trait."

"Unless you call it pushy."

He kept his eyes on her. "You're not pushy."

The waitress reappeared, and set their plates down. Emma cut off a small morsel of the filet, dipped it in the bearnaise, and popped it into her mouth. "Wow, this is incredible. It's been ages since I've had French food."

"Get used to it," he said with a cryptic smile.

She wiped her mouth and laughed. "On my budget, are you kidding?"

"There's a lot of French food in Guernsey."

"You mean…?" She swallowed hard.

He nodded. "Somehow I'm going to get you to Sheldale so you can do your research."

It was too good to be true. "You really think you can get permission for me to go?"

"I think so."

"Oh, John!" If there hadn't been a table full of plates, wine and beef between them, she would have hugged him. "You will come with me, won't you?"

His eyes widened and she could have sworn he said, "Now that would be taking a hell of a chance."

"I beg your pardon?" she asked.

He sipped his wine, then swiped the napkin across

his mouth. "I said, that would be a good chance to get to know you better."

"So you'll come?"

A corner of his mouth twisted upwards, and he shook his head. "I don't think I'll be able to make it. But you don't need me there."

"Yes, I do." She smiled. "It would be so much *fun*. Come on, won't you even consider it?"

"I'll—" He nodded, as if trying to convince someone other than her. "I'll check my schedule, but I can't make any guarantees. Though maybe it would be best if I was there."

She raised an eyebrow. "Best?"

"I mean I know my way around the island a little bit. It might make it a little easier for you."

She smiled. "I'd love it."

"Okay, then." He took a long, deliberate breath and let it out slowly. "I'll see what I can do."

Chapter Three

After that, the conversation flowed easily. Emma was touched by John's enthusiasm to show her his country, to do ordinary British things: finding fish and chips served in paper, riding the train across the countryside, perhaps even going to some of the touristy landmarks, such as Madame Tussaud's wax museum and Kew Gardens.

When they finally left the restaurant, it was after eleven. The hours had slipped by like minutes. "What a night," John commented, as they stepped out into the evening air.

"It's beautiful," Emma agreed. The sky was a dark, translucent purple and only a few wisps of cloud scudded across the face of the moon. The temperature had cooled to warm and balmy. But it wasn't just the weather that she was happy about, it was the company. She'd looked forward to meeting

John for so long that disappointment had seemed practically inevitable.

But she hadn't been disappointed. In fact, Emma would call her feelings for John love at first sight, if she believed in that—which of course she didn't.

"I'll call about Sheldale in the morning," he said, and put his hand on her elbow to guide her across the street.

"I really appreciate it," Emma said, surprised at the thrill she felt at his light touch on her arm.

"I only wish I'd done it sooner," he said, with what sounded like regret. He let go of her arm.

It suddenly felt cold where his hand had been. She dragged her attention back to the conversation. "Stop it, now, John. There's no way you could have known. I certainly don't want you feeling guilty about it."

He gave a concessionary shrug. "All right. I'll call you as soon as I know anything." As he looked for the car key, a shiny black taxicab trundled past, followed by a red double-decker bus.

Emma drank in the atmosphere. "Remember, I don't have a phone in my room, so you have to make sure they go and get me or take the time to take a message."

"No phone in your room?" He opened the car door for her, his gallantry a marked contrast to the tiny cheap car. "Are you serious?"

"Surely this concept isn't new to you?" she said with a smile. "A lot of the small hotels and B and Bs don't have phones in the rooms. Or do you only stay at the Ritz?"

"Almost never," he said, with a straight face.

She got into the car. "Well, the Sunnington Hotel is not exactly luxury, but it's very quaint. I like it."

He got in his side of the car and looked thoughtful as they small-talked on the short drive back to her hotel.

When they got there, he parked—a little awkwardly—and got out to walk her to the door.

"I had such a good time tonight," Emma said, as they approached the door. "Thank you so much."

"Thank *you*," he said earnestly. "You cannot even imagine what tonight has meant to me." He took a step toward her.

For one shuddering moment, they stood face-to-face, looking into each other's eyes. The thought that she should step back, both physically and emotionally, occurred to Emma on some level, but she couldn't move.

With a small smile, he reached out and pulled her into his arms. Against her better judgement, she melted against him, delighting in the feel of his arms around her. She should have told herself to stop, but she couldn't. She wouldn't.

"I've wanted to do this all night." He lowered his mouth onto hers. There was no hesitation, no uncertainty. He moved expertly, parting her lips with his and deepening the kiss to one that made the bones in her legs turn to rubber.

She languished in his embrace, allowing the pleasure to rush over her in dizzying waves. Every sense came to life as she felt him, tasted him, and inhaled the light, spicy scent of his aftershave. It was the last sense she had before succumbing completely to the delight of his kiss.

Just as she was about to lose herself completely in the kiss, he pulled back, leaving her slightly dizzy and wanting more.

"I'd better go now," he said, a bit quickly. It was almost brusque. He must have realized it because his expression softened and he added, "I'll call you first thing in the morning."

"O-okay," she said uneasily. What had just happened? She wasn't sure if it was right or wrong, but it had certainly felt good. Why had he stopped? Perhaps he'd remembered the favor she'd asked and was now feeling put out by it. "Are you sure it's not too much trouble?"

"Not at all. Honestly." He glanced down, then looked back at her. "About that—just now. I apologize for being so forward."

"No...that...don't worry about it." She bit down on her lower lip. This awkwardness was the perfect illustration of why they shouldn't get romantically involved. Their friendship was too valuable to lose to this kind of bumbling chitchat. "Okay, well, good night."

He looked at her for one steady moment. "Good night, Emma." He turned toward the car.

"John," she called after him, before she had time to think what she was doing.

After a moment's pause, he turned back. "Yes?"

That hesitation froze her. She searched her mind for something to say, something that might smooth over the discomfort they were both feeling and put them back on familiar territory. "Drive carefully," was all she could come up with.

He gave a wave of acknowledgment and jumped into the car, pulling out into the street almost the minute the ignition turned over.

Forty minutes later, Emma lay in the dark solitude of her room, shifting on the hard bed. She knew she shouldn't be fantasizing romantically about John, but the images kept coming into her head regardless. The memory of that shivering moment when she looked into his eyes, and then his kiss... She tossed and turned, unable to doze for her pounding heart. She could have run a marathon sooner than fall asleep.

When she had begun planning her trip, she truly hadn't thought there might be any kind of romance in the offing for her and John. She still didn't. But that kiss—while part of her had wanted it all evening—had thrown a wrench in the works. So was the way she was dwelling on it now.

She was probably being swept away by the glamour of being in a foreign country, that was all. And the fact that a man as handsome as a movie star had pulled her into his arms and kissed her passionately. Under any circumstances, she might have found that difficult to resist, but this was John, and what she had with him was more important than anything.

It was simply a temporary lapse of judgment she'd suffered from. Now that she had her wits about her, she knew she wasn't willing to give up the friendship she had with John for a whirlwind romance, no matter how intoxicating it might be. Besides, even if by some wild fluke he wanted to pursue a romantic relationship with her, it wasn't as though it could ever work out. They lived in two different countries, on two different continents. The best they could hope for would be a momentary flame that would fizzle out as soon as they were apart, leaving nothing but a small trail of smoke where their closeness had once been.

Although, there was something strained about their closeness too. For two years she'd read his letters and written to him, without even a hint of self-consciousness. There hadn't seemed to be any self-consciousness on his part either, but tonight he'd been more serious than she'd expected. More somber. Maybe it was just the newness of meeting him in person, but all evening she'd had the nagging sense that his guard was up. Which put *her* guard up and probably made her a lot less fun than he would have hoped. Which made for a question between them that no one had answered. What was wrong? Was he disappointed that she wasn't what he expected her to be?

Or was it jet lag on her part, making her imagine things that weren't there? That had to be it.

Her thoughts quieted, leaving only one small voice which had been there all the time but which had gone unheard. As she drifted into sleep, she heard the voice loud and clear. It wasn't paranoia, it wasn't cynicism... Something important was not right here.

John, the voice said, was hiding something.

Chapter Four

Brice cursed colorfully as he accelerated through the streets of London. He shouldn't have kissed her. They'd been going along just fine, then he'd gone and kissed her and changed the whole slant of their relationship. Damn it, he *wasn't* going to let her friendship go for the sake of a temporary physical pleasure.

But it had been so hard to resist. She'd looked so lovely, so fresh in the night air, so full of enthusiasm for everything around her. Compared to the women he'd dated, she was as refreshing as a cool drink on a steamy day. He'd wanted to drink her in completely.

It was a desire he would have to get under control.

He drew onto the main road and pressed harder on the accelerator. The Mini's lawn-mower engine hummed up to fifty miles per hour.

"Bloody fool," he said, tightening his hands on the wheel. It was bad enough to be lying to her, but to take that step past friendship with her believing him to be John Turnhill would be unconscionable. He let out a long breath and eased up on the accelerator. The car slowed immediately to a more reasonable pace.

What, exactly, *was* it about Emma that he had found so irresistible all evening? What was it that made her seem so much more appealing than the other women he knew? The moment he asked himself the question, a long list of answers came to mind. She was extremely intelligent. She was interesting, too. When she spoke, he didn't want her to stop. He loved her voice. He also loved her eyes. He loved the way she looked at him; a way that made him feel that he was the only man in the world who mattered to her.

And if he wasn't careful he would lose her.

Sexual involvement could *only* lead to disaster. After everything they'd shared, he couldn't imagine making love with her, then returning to just being friends as if nothing had happened. It would always be there, between them, an invisible wedge that would keep them apart where they had previously been closest.

That was it. He'd apologize to her tomorrow. Hopefully it wasn't too late. He turned the car into the driveway of John's home with a jerk. He would rather have gone home, to his house in Kensington, but this was where Emma would call him if she needed him.

When he got inside, he dug out a cheap bottle of port and poured himself a glass. The red liquid burned down his throat and he was glad. He felt guilty for keeping up the charade as John Turnhill. What he should have done when she had told him she was coming to Britain was to tell her he had business in Dublin or something so he couldn't see her while she was here. One more lie, but a lie to protect her.

She would have hated that.

This was the trouble. His logical mind had all the answers—forget it, maintain the friendship, there are other women in the world, you have a role to fulfill and you can't do it with her—yet something about Emma Lawrence made him want to forget all about real life and its obligations. He had an almost over-whelming desire to give up all of his responsibilities and run away with her. Even the thought of her raised an unfamiliar ache in his chest. Like a need.

A need which could never be satisfied.

Brice called Emma early the next morning and told her he'd managed to get permission for her to explore the gardens at Sheldale House. He offered to drive her to Victoria Station to see her off and she accepted, adding that she still wished he would come along.

When he got to her hotel, she was already out front, surrounded by luggage.

"What's all this?" he asked, bending to pick up a bag. "I thought you were only going for a couple of days."

"I am." She hefted a case over her shoulder. "This is my sleeping bag, and that," she indicated the bag he'd just picked up, "is a pup tent."

He stopped. She couldn't be serious. "A sleeping bag and a *pup tent?* Emma, I thought you were joking when you said you'd pitch a tent."

She smiled. "I never joke about pup tents."

Her smile touched him, and he had to squelch a momentary impulse to pull her into his arms. But he had the ominous feeling that there was steely determination behind her words. "I can't let you do this."

"Do what?"

"*This,*" he gestured toward her sleeping bag with the pup tent in his hand. "You can't camp out by yourself in a country you're unfamiliar with."

She looked completely bemused. "Of course I can!"

"Emma, it's not safe." Were there public campgrounds near the house? What were they like? He couldn't remember ever seeing one or even *hearing* about any. All he knew about camping was what he'd seen in old American western movies, and, for a woman especially, it hadn't seemed pleasant.

"Look, John." She smiled again and spoke as if she was explaining something to a small child. "There are a lot of things I'm not prepared to do: attend the opera, go to a state dinner at the White House, use the correct fork for caviar at Buckingham Palace—but to sleep on grass and dirt won't be a problem."

Brice didn't point out that one would use a small spoon for caviar. If he hadn't known better, he would have thought she was aiming those words directly at him. But she couldn't be, she didn't know who he really was. Perhaps she was just trying to reassure him that she wasn't interested in the earl for anything other than his gardens.

She continued. "Put me in high society and I'd be lost. Put me in the wild and I'm perfectly at home. It's part of my job." Her voice softened. "Really, don't worry about me."

He wondered how many people who had said those very words had lived to rue them. "If some psychotic stray approaches you, how are you going to get away when you have to carry all this stuff?"

She laughed. "If a psychotic stray approaches me and I feel I have to run, I'll leave this stuff behind, believe me." She kept smiling. "I'm beginning to see where you're coming from, though. Your instincts are all city. If *you* should ever decide to go camping, I hope you'll take someone like me along." She hoisted a backpack over her other shoulder. "Come on, let's get moving."

He stood still, desperately trying to think of something—*anything*—he could say that might stop her. "What about staying in a hotel? I thought that was the plan."

She shrugged. "You said they'd probably all be full, it being the holiday season and all."

He splayed his arms. "It's worth a *try*, anyway."

"John." She smiled, but there was a strength underlying her tone. "Surely you don't think I'm some helpless woman who can't take care of herself?"

Apparently he was exactly that kind of man. "I

didn't say *helpless*. I just don't understand why you'd take a chance at all."

"I don't think I am taking a chance." She set her backpack down for a moment. "Think about it, how many maidens have you heard of being accosted at campgrounds on Guernsey?"

"The fact that I haven't *heard* of them doesn't mean it hasn't happened or, more to the point, that it couldn't happen."

How quickly could the staff get rid of all evidence of him in Sheldale House, he wondered, then dismissed the thought. They couldn't. There was too much.

Emma shifted her weight and crossed her arms in front of her. "This is a ridiculous conversation, though I appreciate your chivalry."

"No, it's not ridiculous." He'd find a couple of rooms somewhere on Guernsey, that's what he'd do. If only he could figure out how to do *that* without revealing himself to Emma.

She looked at her watch. "The train leaves in an hour, shouldn't we go?"

"Take the later train. First we have to find you a place to stay."

"I've *got* a place to stay." She thumped her sleeping bag.

He narrowed his eyes. "Has anyone ever told you that you're impossibly stubborn?"

She raised her chin. "Not very often."

He couldn't help smiling. "So I bring this out in you?"

"You seem to." A smile came into her eyes.

"Funny, this isn't the sort of thing you can tell from letters, is it?"

His smile froze for a moment. "There's a lot you can't tell from letters."

"I think you're right." She sobered. "But you do know I spend half my life working outdoors. Surely you don't think I'm such a fool that I'll get into trouble camping in England."

He drew air in through his teeth. "Emma, this isn't like America. Things are—things are different here."

"I know, in some ways, things are better. Think about it: the police don't carry guns. It must be *safer* here." She wasn't going to let up, that much was clear. "Let's go now."

She was leaving him no choice. He didn't want to hear about her on the evening news, so he had to do something. There was only one thing that would work. "That's it," he said, practically feeling the tangled web he was weaving cocoon him. "I'm going with you."

Brice's predicament was getting more and more ridiculous by the minute. He couldn't believe he was going to Guernsey, to his own estate, while pretending to be someone else. It went against everything he believed in. He was an honest man, damn it, yet with the one person in the world who mattered most to him, he was being completely dishonest. It was an unreal situation. Every time she called him "John," he felt a painful stab of guilt.

"John." Emma tapped his arm.

There it was again. "Yes?" How many times had

she said it this time before he'd heard? "Sorry, I was somewhere else." *Someone else.*

She gave him a brief look of query, then unfolded a pamphlet she'd picked up at one of the tourist stations. "According to this schedule, if we take the regular ferry from Poole to Guernsey it will take longer, but it will cost a lot less than taking the hydrofoil." The paper was crinkled back into a square. "What do you think?"

"It's a slow boat," he warned, privately thinking he could use the extra time to try and collect himself. "Do you have a problem with seasickness?"

She made a face. "The English Channel is hardly the open sea."

"That's exactly what it is."

She waved her hand. "Oh come on, how bad could it be? People swim across it."

"Not many." He was beginning to realize that Emma Lawrence was pretty stubborn. "It can be fairly rough. Though I suppose if it was bad enough we could have them turn around and we could take another way."

"Have them turn around for us?" Emma laughed. "Your job must give you much more power than I imagined if you're used to having such command."

She had no idea. He hadn't been kidding, but it was lucky she assumed he was. What could he say now? How could he have made such an insanely stupid blunder? "I only meant if there was some sort of...emergency." This was going nowhere.

"Somehow I don't think they'd do that," she said with a shrug and a lingering query in her eyes. "But don't worry about me. I think I can handle a little hop across the channel.'' She nudged him with her elbow. ''But if you're afraid you're going to be seasick, we can go the other way.''

He suspected she might rue her words, but the ferry from Poole left sooner and they were both eager to get going—she to begin, and he to get it over with. He'd already delayed the day by more than an hour when he'd decided to join her. He'd gone back to John's house and hastily thrown some things into an old suitcase he'd found in a cupboard. Since Emma was with him, he'd hurried, taking only a moment to go into another room and call his housekeeper at Sheldale House and hastily explain to her what was happening. He had nearly asked her to take the pictures down but decided it would be easier to keep Emma away from the house than to make his entire household staff understand such a seemingly bizarre request.

A tight knot forced its way into his chest. The rules of this game he was playing were getting too difficult to follow. It was beginning to feel as if he were damned no matter what he did.

Emma had never felt so sick in her life. The boat rocked wildly as it crossed the choppy waters of the channel. White-capped waves crashed against the hull, threatening to swallow it whole. A light sea breeze wafted in through the open doorway to the deck, but it was neither strong enough nor cool enough to do much good for Emma's hot spells.

I think I can handle a little hop across the channel.

Her words came back to haunt her. She hoped he didn't remember her arrogant pronouncement. Now, not only was she sick, but she was almost positive that they were going to be drowned in the dark, churning water because the boat was surely going to go down.

"Didn't one of these boats flip over in the channel a few years ago?" Emma asked, wondering why she had forgotten that incident when they were trying to decide which route to take to the island.

She was lying on a stiff iron bench and John was sitting next to her. Other passengers were similarly situated, or draped awkwardly over the iron seating that was part of the ferry boat.

John looked at her and shrugged. "Probably. They're quite unseaworthy, you know. We might as well be clinging to driftwood."

Emma groaned and rolled over.

"I'm joking, Emma."

"There's the John I know and love." She caught her breath the moment she heard the words come out of her mouth and continued quickly, hoping he hadn't heard the word *love* and panicked. "But, boy, did you pick a great time to finally get light-hearted." She gave a weak smile. "Seriously, you look like you're on top of the world. What's your secret?"

He gave a shrug. "The sea air, I guess. I hadn't realized how confined I felt back in London."

There was a moment of calm in which she surveyed him. He *did* seem to be loosening up. Did the sea air really have that effect on some people? Could a place as wonderful as London really suck the life out of a person that way?

The boat surged and Emma gasped.

He laid a hand on her shoulder. "We're as safe as can be here. They've been doing this for years and years, you know. Don't worry about a thing. Let's go to the window so you can keep your eye on the horizon. That always helps with seasickness."

"I'm not sick." A wave of nausea welled within her and she was silent for a few minutes.

"Can I get you anything?" John asked her after a bit. "How about a cola? Perhaps I could find some crackers."

She nodded weakly. "That would be great. Even a piece of bread."

He stood and walked away. She noted his sure-footed gait, and how easily he adapted his footing to the unpredictable rises and falls of the boat—like an experienced sailor. He wouldn't lose his lunch and make a fool of himself in front of everyone. She wished she could say the same about herself.

He came back with a lukewarm soft drink and a bag of potato chips. "It was the best I could do." He smiled for a moment, then bent down to examine her more closely. "You're really not looking well at all."

I'm going to be sick, she thought suddenly. "I think I'll pop into the bathroom for a moment," she said, taking a soothing gulp of the opened soda. Her effort to sound light and casual had failed miserably. "Just splash a little cold water on my face..." She didn't finish, but somehow managed to stand.

He was beside her in a flash. "Can I walk you there?" He touched her elbow to guide her.

"No," she said quickly. "I'll be right back." She hurried as fast as she could to the bathroom. The embarrassment would hit her full force later. For now, all her energy went to keeping her throat closed. She passed two men sitting casually on the steps, leaning back with half-shut eyes. A three-quarters-empty bottle of vodka sat between them. Emma's stomach lurched again.

Whether it was the soda or the movement, she didn't know, but by the time she stumbled into the tiny bathroom, she was actually feeling better. After taking several deep breaths, she looked in the mirror. It was disheartening, to say the least. She looked ghastly; more yellow than pale, and with blotchy skin. Her hair was the definition of lank and there wasn't a thing she could do about it. The only things available to her were the toilet and the sink, so she turned on the water and splashed some cool water on her face. It helped. She rubbed her cool, damp hands across her forehead and the back of her neck, then took a deep breath. She might just make it after all.

When she got back to John, he was resting. And he looked great, unlike her. Lucky son of a gun, she thought. Yet there had been something very touching about how he'd wanted to take care of her, and how capable he'd seemed of doing so. She'd never considered herself a woman who needed a man to take care of her, and she still didn't, but she'd never taken the time to stop and think how nice it might be to have one every once in a while.

John was making her stop and think a lot of things she'd never thought before.

She sat down next to him and he started.

"You all right?" he asked, immediately on alert.

"Fine." She smiled. There was that kindness again. Under the same circumstances she wondered if she would have had the kindness—or the stomach—to escort a very nauseous person with no sense of balance anywhere.

"We're almost there now," he said, relaxing back against the iron wall of the boat. "I can hear the gulls."

She listened. Outside the open doorway she could hear the faint squawks of seagulls. More importantly, the boat didn't seem to be rocking so wildly anymore. "The channel is a little calmer now, too, isn't it?"

"The closer we get to shore, yes."

"Thank goodness."

He smiled at her and reached for her hand. "Let's go on deck, the fresh air will probably do you some good."

She stood up beside him. "And failing that, I can just lean over the railing." She hesitated. "I hope I'm kidding."

"You'll be fine."

She walked a little unsteadily by his side, up a short flight of potentially slick metal steps and out onto the deck.

A salty wind blew through their hair and rustled their clothing as they made their way to the rail. In the distance, Emma could see land. "Is that Guernsey?"

His eyes were fastened on the horizon. "That's it."

"How much longer do you think it will take?"

He squinted at the land ahead and considered. "Half an hour. Forty-five minutes at the outside."

Excitement rattled through her. She was really going to see the Sheldale gardens. Before long she would be examining the St. Paul's Heart firsthand. "I can't wait to get there," she said.

"You don't have to wait much longer." He looked at her with an expression she couldn't quite read. Was it trepidation she saw in his eyes?

She leaned back and regarded him. "Why do you look so serious?"

"Do I?"

"Sort of."

He looked as though he were going to speak, then stopped. When he spoke, his words seemed measured. "Emma, I enjoy being with you."

"But?"

"But what?"

"It sounded like there was a 'but' coming." She looked him over. It occurred to her then that he sounded like that a lot. Since they'd met—even since they'd spoken on the phone—there was a reserve about him that surprised her. The man she'd been writing to for two years was light, funny and easygoing, yet in person he was, well, a little stiff. *Reserved* might be a better word. And, as she'd said, very serious.

"No," he said, watching her closely. "No qualifying. If anything, I'm not used to taking off on vacation at the last minute this way."

There it was again. The John on paper didn't seem like the kind of guy who had to plan every move in advance. He'd seemed carefree, spontaneous. Not that she minded the difference. In fact, it added an interesting dimension to him. She'd met plenty of men who were willing to live for the pleasure of the moment, but very few who had the maturity and dignity she saw under John's surface. "You're a little different than I thought you'd be," she said aloud.

His eyes widened for a moment, then his cool veil of reserve returned. "In what way?"

"Well," she frowned, "you're very quiet sometimes. I mean you're just…deeper, I guess, than I expected. Not that I thought you were shallow, of course." She shrugged. This wasn't coming out right at all. She was insulting him, and she didn't know how to get back on the right track. "But you're serious one minute, then light-hearted the next, without any rhyme or reason to it."

He gave a nod and looked back to the land. "You make me manic, in a way."

"Me?"

He turned to her and smiled. "Yes. You bring something different out in me. But it feels good." He looked surprised at his own words, then repeated, "It does feel good."

Her face flushed with pleasure. "There's a lot of stuff going on under the surface with you, John Turnhill."

He gave a laugh that didn't quite reach his eyes. Whatever light-heartedness she might have brought out in him went right back inside. "The problem with looking for things under the surface is that you might not like what you find."

She raised an eyebrow. "Deep, dark secrets?"

"Worse." A faint smile touched his lips, but his eyes grew more serious than ever. "An ordinary man."

St. Peter Port was bustling with activity. As they walked through the winding streets, it was almost like something from a fairy tale. The pastel and white stone buildings that surrounded them under the pale blue skies were as pretty as a Monet painting. Brice wondered why it had been so long since he'd last come to visit. *You're so serious,* Emma had said. Emma and the rest of the world. Perhaps they were right. He'd become so caught up in the mundane details of his life that he hadn't bothered to notice the incredible beauty available to him. Sheldale House was his ancestral home, yet coming here had long felt like a vacation from reality, and he wasn't able to afford the luxury of such a vacation. He had a company to run, after all, important things to do.

He almost couldn't believe he was here now. Moreover, he couldn't believe the thrum of excitement in his chest at the familiar sights and sounds. He didn't remember the last time he'd felt this way. It must be because of Emma oohing and aahing at everything by his side. In the light of her enthusiasm, everything glowed.

Everything except, perhaps, for him. She'd obviously noticed he wasn't quite the person he'd been on paper. Well, what had he expected? He was no actor, he couldn't just pretend to be something he wasn't. Although wasn't that what he'd been doing in writing these past two years?

He dismissed the thought. Everything he'd written, every feeling he'd described and every desire he'd touched upon, had been absolutely authentic. He'd reached into a part of him that was very private, but it was him nevertheless. The problem was that he'd done it under someone else's name.

Now he just had to see the charade through. Somehow. The lie had got out of control, but he couldn't disappoint her by telling her the truth. He just couldn't shred her faith that way. She'd been through enough in her life already. Perhaps the best thing would be to see this through now, to let her finish her trip in peace, and then gradually to sever their ties after she was gone. Would that hurt her less than finding out how he'd deceived her? He thought so. He hoped so.

But letting go would be very hard for him. He looked at Emma's profile as she walked beside him. Just looking at her made his chest tighten. She was so important to him. How could he ever let her go?

He wasn't sure he could.

They found a call box on a side street, and Brice decided that now wasn't the time to think about the future. There was plenty of time for that later. *Now* he had to find a way to make it through the next few days without deepening his involvement with Emma, and thereby making everything more difficult.

He lifted the telephone receiver and sent a silent prayer that he would be able to find a hotel. It didn't look good. He made a couple of calls to hotels he knew to be reputable, but every place he could think of was full. It was the height of the tourist season, and not a room was to be had. At least not for John Turnhill, and with Emma standing beside him that was the only name he could use.

Finally he found a hotel in St. Peter Port that, a moment before he'd called, had had one cancellation.

"We have one room," the cheery hotel clerk said. "With a full-sized bed, so it sleeps two. It has a marvelous view of the sea."

One room. One bed. Impossible. "No, you don't understand. We need two rooms." Brice took a step, turning slightly away from Emma so that she couldn't see his face.

And so that he couldn't see hers.

"I do apologize," the voice said on the other end of the line, impatient now. "We only have the one."

Brice sighed. "Look, are you sure you don't have something else? Even a broom closet somewhere?"

"John!" Emma tapped insistently on his arm. "Take the room. We can share."

He turned to face her, raising his eyebrows for confirmation of what she'd just said. Things had been bad enough the other night when he'd kissed her, how could he share a room with her without facing irresistible temptation? Even her hand on his arm now made him want to sweep her into his arms and carry her to a hotel room. If he got any more involved with Emma while pretending to be John Turnhill, he would probably roast in hell.

"Yes," she whispered insistently, unaware of how her touch affected him. "Take the room. If it's all we can get, let's get it before it's gone. You made me leave my tent in London, remember."

Visions of sharing a bed tonight flew to mind, and Brice gave himself a mental shake. He'd take the floor, of course. Or sleep on a wooden chair in the lobby. He'd do whatever he had to. Just because he was, in a sense, living a lie didn't mean he had the right to behave dishonorably. "Yes, then, I'll take the room," he said brusquely into the phone.

"And what is your name, sir?"

"The name is Pal—" He paused for a fit of coughing. Really, he was going to have to be more careful. He'd almost given it away that time. "Turnhill. John Turnhill."

"Mr. and Mrs?"

"What?" He frowned. "Mr. and Mrs?" Brice felt his face grow warm.

The voice continued, not waiting for an answer. "All right, Mr. Turnhill, we'll expect you and your wife this afternoon."

"Oh, er, fine. Thank you." He replaced the receiver and took a long breath before turning to face Emma. "It's set," he said, with the finality of a death pronouncement.

"Good." She looked relieved. "I was beginning to think we wouldn't be able to find shelter anywhere."

He thought of Sheldale House. "It was looking grim, that's for certain."

"Besides, it will be fun to be your wife for a couple of days."

The words sent an undefined emotion through his chest. "Don't worry, I'll set them straight on that when we get there."

"Why bother? I think it's kind of a kick. And you know if you tell them we're not married, they'll immediately jump to the wrong conclusions about what we'll be doing in the room." She glanced at him. "If you know what I mean."

He knew what she meant all right. "We wouldn't want your virtue called into question," he said with a laugh.

She slanted a gaze at him that made his stomach tighten. "Or yours."

They began walking down the old cobbled sidewalk, and Brice thought with every step that he was getting in deeper and deeper. He had to take control.

"What a beautiful day," Emma said dreamily.

"Emma." Brice's voice weakened and he tried again. "Emma."

"Mmm?" She stopped in front of a newsagent's stand, and idly picked up a newspaper. He saw a reference to a story about Palliser Telecommunications on the cover. His lie was going to catch up with him, he knew it. "I'm not sure this is a good idea," he said, fighting the urge to rip the paper from her hands and wad it up into a ball.

Fortunately she put the paper back herself, and

turned very serious eyes upon him. "What's not a good idea?"

"Sharing a room." He sounded like a prude and he hated it. But the alternative was worse—he couldn't give in to any midnight temptation with Emma, especially while she believed he was John Turnhill. He also couldn't tell her the truth.

"Is it that terrible?"

Worse. "The problem is—" He stopped, noticing the newsagent's eyes upon him. He turned away, taking Emma by the arm. "The problem is that I don't want to make you uncomfortable. There's only one bed."

She hesitated for a fraction of a minute, then said, "We're grown-up people, John. I think we can manage. Unless *you're* that uncomfortable with the idea…?"

"No, it's not *me* I'm worried about," he said quickly. "It's you."

She stopped. "Me?"

That hadn't come out right. "I mean, it must be awkward for you to suddenly find yourself having to share a small hotel room with a man you don't know all that well." Although not half as awkward as it was for him to be protective about such things. "Not that anything would happen to compromise you…."

Her expression shifted almost imperceptibly. "Of course not. I trust you, John. We're good friends. Surely we can share a room for a few days without feeling strange about it. Especially if it's the only way to get to Sheldale House."

He tried to reassure her. "Believe me, if there was

any other way..." He let the statement trail off. There was nothing else to say.

"Don't worry about it," she said, brushing it off. "I'd sleep in a bathtub or a tree or wherever I had to in order to look at the gardens."

He nodded dully.

She took a deep breath and slapped her hands down at her sides. "Now stop worrying about little details like my virtue, and let's check into that room before the hotel gives it away."

The hotel was French, run by one of the many Gallic settlers on the island. It was called L'Hotel du Notre Dame, and after wandering the winding streets for twenty minutes they finally found it next to a small church, with a high steeple and a bell that glistened in the sunlight. Across the street there was a broad marina. She could hear the gentle creak of the ships' riggings as they bobbed on the waves.

They stepped into a cool, dark hotel lobby that was surprisingly elegant. It was far more upscale than she had anticipated.

"Are you sure this is the place?" Emma asked, suddenly self-conscious about her faded jeans and wrinkled cotton shirt.

"This is it," he said simply. "You relax a moment, I'll check in."

He left Emma to admire the oil paintings on the lobby wall while he went to get the keys from the desk. It seemed to take a very long time, but when she tried to hear what they were saying, she realized they were not only speaking in low voices but also in French. She wondered why she was surprised that John spoke French. It seemed there were a lot of surprising things about him.

Finally, the desk clerk handed a gleaming over-sized key to John and gave Emma a pleasant nod and a wink.

"Ready?" John asked her.

She nodded and they walked to the elevator. It was the cage kind that she'd seen in a thousand old movies. John slid the fancy black iron door back and waited for Emma to enter.

"This is...really fancy," she said, watching the opulently decorated floors pass.

"Yes, I meant to speak to you about that." He cleared his throat and shifted uncomfortably. "I've already covered the cost of the room—"

"John, you can't—"

He held up a hand. "I knew you'd object, but I really must insist. If I had done things differently you wouldn't be paying for accommodations anyway."

She frowned. He was right, she could have camped for free. But that didn't mean he should have to foot the bill for this kind of luxury. "John, this place must cost a fortune."

He smiled and her heart tripped. "Not your worry, Emma." The elevator stopped and he opened the cage door.

As they walked down the long hallway toward room 404, the overhead lights lit their way before them and dimmed behind them. Emma looked up in amazement. "Are these lights motion sensitive?"

John nodded and stopped in front of their door.

"It's more economical—they don't have to burn lights all day and night when no one is using them."

It may have been a matter of economics for the hotel but it felt like magic to Emma. "I feel a little like I'm in an enchanted castle," she said, still looking at the hall, even though he'd opened the door. Never in her life had she stayed in a hotel as nice as this.

She walked into the room slowly, in awe of the simple yet luxurious surroundings. There were high ceilings with exposed beams, a carved wooden dresser that held a vase of fresh white roses, wide picture windows revealing a span of the sea, with tall ships and their watercolor reflections on the glassy water. In the corner there was a glass cabinet housing several leather-bound books and expensive-looking crystal figures.

And of course, there was the bed.

It was considerably smaller than her American mind had imagined it would be. Somehow she'd pictured a half-acre king-sized bed with plenty of room for modesty. A million movies had used the same device, always with the couple hanging a sheet from the ceiling to divide them. This bed was scarcely larger than a twin bed, and it was difficult to imagine two people being in it without touching each other.

John must have been thinking the same thing because, behind her, he said, "I'll sleep on the floor."

"You don't have to do that." Her objection was weaker than she'd wanted it to be. The idea of touching John held an appeal that was disconcerting to Emma. In fact, since they'd kissed the night before, she'd had a great many disconcerting thoughts about John.

"Yes, I do." He plopped her suitcase onto the stand at the end of the bed, then put his own on the dresser and rummaged through it. "I don't know about you," he said, "but I'm in dire need of a shower. Would you mind?"

She shook her head and gestured toward the bathroom. "Go right ahead." So now he'd be naked just a few feet away, on the other side of the door. That wasn't helping her keep her thoughts platonic. "In fact, I think I'll pop down to the corner and get a local newspaper."

She could have sworn he grimaced, but he said, "All right then," and gave a nod before turning toward the bathroom.

It wasn't until she heard the water running that she took her purse and went back out the door and down to the street exit opposite the lobby. Truthfully she wanted a shower herself, but she was too self-conscious to say so. Silly. She was a capable woman in just about every other endeavor, but when it came to dealing with men, she was hopeless.

She lingered at the corner kiosk for a moment after choosing a newspaper, and picked out a candy bar as well. She ate it on the way back up to the room.

When she walked in, John stood with his back to her, a white towel wrapped around his narrow waist. His dark hair was glossy and wet, and little drops of shower water still gleamed on his shoulders and back. He turned to face her, and she saw that his suitcase was on the stand in front of him, open to reveal neatly folded clothes. "Sorry." He grabbed some clothes from the case and went back to the steamy bathroom. "I thought you'd...I'll only be a moment. Did you want to use the shower?"

She met his eyes and swallowed hard. "N-no. No, thanks. I'll do it later." Her heart pounded foolishly. For heaven's sake, it wasn't as though he was indecent or anything. You could see more skin on a construction worker on the street outside the lab almost any day in the summer, yet the sight of John's muscular back gave her thoughts that would have shocked her childhood Sunday-school teacher.

He nodded. "I'll just go back in and change then," he said, walking into the smaller room.

The tension in the air was thicker than the steam.

"Okay." Emma turned her gaze to the window and pretended to be interested in something she saw outside.

The door closed and John said, "Do you want to get some dinner?"

"I'd really like to get to Sheldale House," she called back, grateful for something neutral to discuss. "Maybe we could just pick up some sandwiches and take them with us. There's probably at least another hour or so of daylight." She leaned against the window sill. "What about the earl?"

There was a bang in the bathroom, followed by a sharp utterance. "What about him?"

"Will he be there? I'm not too clear on how you arranged this. Do we have to check in with someone? Curtsy?" She was smiling as she said it, but she wasn't altogether sure that wouldn't be expected.

The door opened and John came out, looking devastatingly handsome in faded jeans and a pale blue T-shirt. "No, we can just go walk around the grounds."

Emma clicked her tongue against her teeth. "Shoot. I forgot a trowel. It's with my tent."

John nodded. "Doesn't matter. All that stuff is there."

She raised an eyebrow. "And the earl of Palliser won't mind us helping ourselves to it?"

"Not at all." He looked at her and smiled. "He's actually a very generous man."

"I hope you're right about that because I sure don't want to incur an earl's wrath." She tossed her suitcase on the bed and went about unpacking. When she got to her underwear, she hesitated, embarrassed to toss the lacy objects into the drawer while he watched her. At that point, though, it would have been equally awkward to leave them in the suitcase deliberately, so she dropped them into the drawer.

John looked away discreetly.

"Do you think the maid will be alarmed if I leave these out?" she asked with a laugh, producing a package of biodegradable seeding pots. "I don't want her to think I'm doing any kind of illegal farming in here."

He looked at them. "What are those?"

She held up the package. "For cuttings."

"Cuttings?"

"Of the St. Paul's Heart. I figure I can take five or six cuttings back to the States and that should ensure us enough plants to begin studying."

He nodded. "Is that legal or are you going to have to go through a lot of red tape?"

"The lab takes care of all that, fortunately." She dropped the pack into a large shoulder bag and slung it onto her back. "Ready?"

"I guess so." He smiled, though she also noticed him taking a deep breath.

"All right," she said, barely containing her excitement. "Let's go to Sheldale House."

Chapter Five

Earl Palliser's Sheldale House was even more beautiful than Emma had imagined from the few photos she'd seen. They'd rented a car in town and driven up a shaded country lane into a long driveway. The wrought-iron gates outside the estate were open and inviting. The pounded-dirt driveway wound around through acres of twisted birch trees, dogwoods and weeping willows. Then, suddenly, the foliage gave way to a long, lush sweep of green lawn. There, looming before them in the distance, was the house. Only it was much more than a house. It was like a grand old Newport mansion, made of millions of sun-bleached stones. Emma guessed that there were more than fifty windows on the face of the house alone.

John's photos had been good, but there was no way a photograph could capture the splendor of the ancient house rising high against the pale sky of twilight. The setting sun sent shadows slanting sharply across the building's facade, making the pointed eaves seem even more dramatic and Gothic than they would have in full sunlight. Rich green ivy covered parts of the deep-red building like a shawl draped delicately over a woman's shoulders. Behind the house to the west, green lawn swept away in gently rolling hills. To the south, the garden was a burst of color so vivid and so varied that it called fireworks to Emma's mind. She sat very still, taking it all in.

"It's magnificent," she said, in a rush of breath. "How could he ever leave this place?"

John drew the car to a halt and took off his seat belt. "Who?"

"The earl of Palliser," Emma said, getting out of the car and taking a deep breath of the sweet air. Birds whistled bright songs in the distance. It was like an illustration from a children's book, perhaps *The Secret Garden,* come to life. "You said he's away a lot. If I lived here, I'd never want to leave."

"Really?" He sounded surprised, and she had the sense that he was neither hearing nor seeing the same Sheldale House that she was. They began walking across the grass. "I would have thought this was far too cold and austere for your taste."

She turned to him in disbelief. "*Cold?* Are you kidding? Look at this." She swept her arm across the scene before them. "Can you imagine how much love and care went into cultivating all of this? Generations and generations of gardeners have put their hearts and souls into this creation."

He followed her gesture but didn't look impressed. "It's their job."

She smiled and shook her head. He didn't have a clue. "*Weeding* is their job. *Planting* is their job. Creating something like this is a labor of love, believe me."

He continued to look at the sweep of lawn for a moment in silence. "I never thought about it before," he eventually said softly.

She shrugged. "No, most people don't. And, really, why would you have? It's not like you live here and take it for granted. Most people see a place like this and think it's nice, it's pretty, but they don't think very far beyond that. I see this and I think it's a work of art. A masterpiece"

"I'm glad you appreciate it that way."

"Oh, I do." She took a hearty breath, drinking in as much of the beauty as she could. "Okay. Where did you take the picture?"

"Picture?" For a moment he looked baffled, then realization came into his eyes. "Oh, right. It's...it's this way." After looking around for a moment, he started toward the explosion of flowers.

As they walked, Emma gaped at her surroundings, unable to shake her awe of the place. "So, all of this belongs to just one man?"

He nodded. "One family." He glanced around, as though they might run into one of them at any moment. "But there aren't many members of the Palliser family left, so I guess you could say it's the responsibility of one man. One of many responsibilities, which is why he doesn't come here very often."

"That's a shame. Does he have any children?"

John gave a sharp laugh. "*Children?* What makes you ask that?"

She wondered why the question brought such a strong reaction from John but didn't ask. "This would be a great place for kids to grow up."

He gave her a dark look. "You must be joking."

"I'm not. What could be better than growing up with this—this vast spread around you?"

"It's vast all right." His mouth set in a hard line. "It could make you feel very small."

She laughed at the cynicism of his reaction. "Wow, you really are a pessimist. I think this would be a wonderful place for kids to play. Fresh air, acres and acres of lawn to run on, deep, dark gardens to hide in. It would be great."

He grimaced, but kept his gaze straight ahead. "You may be idealizing a bit."

From what she'd heard about aristocratic childhoods, he was probably right. "Still, if *I* lived here, I would make sure it was a warm place, not a cold one."

A strange look came into his eyes as he stopped and regarded her. "I believe you would."

They reached a high row of boxwoods and Emma was grateful for the change of subject. "What's this, a maze?"

He barely looked at it. "Yes."

"Let's go through it."

He hung back. "I thought you wanted to get to the St. Paul's Heart?"

She smiled and gave him a pat on the back. "For

heaven's sake, John, we *can* take a moment to stop and smell the roses. Literally.''

He hesitated, then took a short breath and said, "All right." He gestured for her to enter before him.

She started onto the worn brick path. "Have you been in here before?"

"Not in years."

She stopped and turned to him. "How long ago did you take the pictures for the book?"

He shifted his weight and glanced around again. "Those were taken about four years ago, I guess."

"That's not so long." She began walking again, idly trailing her finger along the wall of foliage beside her. "I doubt it's changed that much in four years."

"No, probably not."

She rounded a corner and then another one, reveling in the cool green scent of the earth and boxwoods. "Shoot, we've just gone in a circle." She turned to him and laughed. "See? Isn't this fun?"

"Actually," he took a step toward her, his presence easing into hers as naturally as if they were one, "it's different, seeing it through your eyes." He stopped, then added softly, "It's nice."

A thrill trickled over her like cool water. "So you're glad you came?"

He gave a devastating smile and pointed a finger at her. "You like to be right, don't you, Ms. Lawrence?"

She felt the warm flush sweep over her face. "That's not the point. Are you?"

He touched the tip of her nose, then her chin. "Yes, I'm glad I came."

She swallowed. "I'm glad you did too." She wondered if he was going to kiss her. She held her breath, hoping he would, and tilted her face up to his.

He paused before her, and for one shivering moment she could feel him coming toward her. Then suddenly the mood changed. He stepped back and looked at the sky, his green eyes paled to gray in the evening light. Emma's heart did a flip. "It's getting darker now," he warned in a low voice. She realized all at once that she loved his voice. "We should go find your plant."

"Right. Okay," she managed.

They traipsed in silence across half an acre to a small glen that Emma recognized from the book. There were tall oak trees in a row and next to that was a large patch of marigolds and the coveted St. Paul's Heart. Emma gasped at the sight of it. There was even more than she'd realized. She walked slowly to the patch and knelt before it, taking one of the tender stems between her thumb and forefinger.

"That's the stuff right there, isn't it?" John asked behind her.

"This is it," she said, pinching the thick chive-like stem. It tore and a small drop of fluid came out on her finger. She lifted it to her nose and smelled the odd citrus-like scent. It was unlike anything she could name. "This is it," she repeated, more softly. "I can't believe it." Tears stung her eyes. Finally, after all this time she had the opportunity to study this rare plant. To take it back to the lab and analyze it firsthand. She took a pad out of her bag and began making notes on the environment, the surrounding plants, the shade-to-light proportion, and the size of the patch.

John watched in silence for a few minutes, then said, "Would you like me to find someone to dig some of this up for you?"

She shook her head. "I'll do it."

"Yourself?"

She smiled and returned the pad to her bag. "Well, you can help." She pulled out the planting pots. "But we do need some trowels and maybe a box or something to set them in."

He glanced in the direction of a potting shed. "I'll get them for you."

"Thanks." She watched him go and wondered why he kept glancing around the way he did. It seemed ever so slightly paranoid. Had he really gotten permission for them to come, or had he just taken pity on her and decided to take a chance on not getting caught?

No way; John was far too principled to do something so sneaky. He was, she was learning, too responsible for that kind of thing. It was probably just her imagination.

He came back five minutes later with two trowels and a sturdy wooden crate. "You'll have to tell me how to do this," he said, handing her one of the trowels. "How deep do we go?"

She stuck the trowel into the ground below a section of the plant, and pulled it up with about two inches of dirt to spare beneath the roots. "Like this," she said, carefully setting it into one of the pots. "Just make sure you don't hit the roots." She put some extra dirt in and patted it down.

"Right." Gingerly, he set about digging below the roots as she had done.

They worked side by side in silence for a few minutes. After she'd taken three samples, Emma sat back and wiped her forehead with the back of her hand. The purple in the sky was deepening, and the sun was nearly down to the horizon. It was unspeakably beautiful. "Let's look around some more," she said, standing and stretching.

"What about the plants?"

"We've got enough now." She reached down for his hand. "Come on, let's explore." She pulled and he stood beside her.

He hung back, emotionally if not physically. "What's to explore?"

"I don't know, everything. How about here?" She pointed into the darkening woods. "Boy, you could get completely lost in here, couldn't you?"

"You can't go too far," John said. He moved beside her and his arm brushed against her shoulder. "You'd get to the edge of the island eventually."

They walked into the shade of the oaks. "I wonder who else has walked on this very spot over the years."

"You'd be surprised," he murmured, then cleared his throat. "We both would, I'm sure. Victor Hugo lived on Guernsey, for instance. Maybe he was here once."

"Or maybe there were knights and damsels in distress. It feels very medieval in here. Magical."

That made him laugh. *"Magical?"*

"Yes, magical." She went to an enormous oak. The base must have had a diameter of about four and a half feet, and it was hollow at the bottom. She poked her head in and was surprised at the space inside. "Look at this, it's like Christopher Robin's house."

John smiled, caught by her excitement. "I used to hide in there as a child. You can put your legs on either side of the opening and no one can see you from the outside."

She stilled, then slowly pulled out, and turned to him, frowning. "You were here as a *child?"*

Damn it. He should have known he'd make that kind of slip. It had been an accident waiting to happen. He'd gotten too comfortable with Emma, too caught up in her enthusiasm. He was bound to trip up. "A tree like that, I mean," he said quickly. "You know, a big oak with a knotted base like that."

That seemed to satisfy her. She nodded and ran her hand along the opening. "I guess there are a lot of old oaks in England. Sherwood Forest is full of them."

"Exactly."

She took his arm and led him back out of the woods. "Let's go peek at the house."

An objection lodged in his throat, but he didn't voice it. Already he was sounding like a finicky puffball, instead of the carefree, adventurous, devil-may-care person he'd been in his letters. He didn't want to make it worse by becoming a schoolmarm, saying they *shouldn't* do this and *couldn't* do that. So he followed her, heavy-limbed, as she bounded toward the house like a puppy.

She stopped in front of the ornate iron gate to the terrace and slipped off her shoes. "Should we tiptoe over and look in?" she asked, her eyes dancing.

He glanced at the window. A faint light shone through, meaning the lights were on in the hallway. Someone could see them out here at any moment. He wondered who was inside and whether he could signal them somehow if they did spot Emma and him. He'd told the housekeeper already in his phone call that he didn't want to be acknowledged if she saw him, but she hadn't understood the instructions very well. In fact, she'd acted as if he was crazy, so he doubted she'd have been able to pass them along adequately to the rest of the staff. That thought had been plaguing him ever since he and Emma had arrived. He worried that at any moment someone might round a corner and give a startled, *Good evening, Lord Palliser, I didn't realize you'd come home.*

Emma was waiting for a response. His instincts told him to leave, to take her to a nice, safe restaurant in town. However, those were the same instincts that he'd followed all his life. The same instincts that made him, by many accounts, the coldest blue blood in Britain. Ignoring the warning bells that went off in his head, he opened the gate and gave a gallant bow. "After you."

She gave a nod and went through the gate, across

the old stone terrace to the window. "Gosh, it's like a palace," she said, her breath fogging the window slightly. She turned to face him. "Have you ever been in there?"

He nodded mutely.

She looked back in. "Is it glorious?"

"It's...old."

She was too enamored at what she was seeing to argue with his assessment. "I think this is some sort of dance hall. I mean *ballroom.*" She narrowed her eyes and crinkled her nose. "What is all that stuff?"

He went and looked in the window beside her. Indeed, the normally bare ballroom was loaded with tables and chairs. They probably had a major cleaning project of some sort going on inside.

"I'm not sure," he said.

"I bet it's glorious when it's all lit up for a party," Emma breathed. "That is, if they still have parties here. Do they?"

"Not for a long time."

She faced him. "That's sad, don't you think?"

It was on the tip of his tongue to point out how impractical it would be to have an old-style ball there, how much it would cost to cater and decorate and light it, how much planning would have to go into creating a guest list and menu...but that was the practical Brice. There was another side to him, a side that agreed with Emma that it could be interesting— perhaps even fun—to do what she suggested. He tried to think what he'd say if he was writing to her instead of standing before her.

She beat him to it. "Care to dance?"

He raised an eyebrow. "Here?"

"Why not?"

The man he wanted to be would have said the exact same thing. "Why not," he agreed, and took her hand.

"It's too bad we don't have a radio or something."

That gave him just the chance he needed. "We don't need a radio." He put a finger to his lips. "Can't you hear the music?"

She frowned and appeared to listen. "No."

He met her eyes and smiled. This other part of him *did* come rather easily, when he let it. "You have to listen very closely."

Understanding came into her eyes. "Ah, I think I hear it now."

He put his arm around her waist and pulled her close.

She took a quick breath as her body touched his. "I believe that's *The Blue Danube Waltz.* Or is it Bob Marley?" She gave a laugh. "It's so hard to tell from here."

He smiled down at her, feeling happiness at Sheldale House for perhaps the first time in his life. "It's whatever you want it to be."

Slowly they began to move, their feet shuffling softly against the rough flagstones of the terrace. In the distance night birds began to sing. For one crazy moment, he almost thought he did hear music.

She followed his lead, and they swayed gently across the patio, perfectly in tune with each other and the music in their hearts. The sky had grown dark but glowed already with early evening stars.

Then without warning the outside lights clicked on, illuminating the path through the garden.

Emma gasped. "Look at that, it's like little fairy lights."

Brice laughed and tightened his hold on her waist. She brought something out in him that didn't exist before. He was practically drunk with it. "You're a very romantic soul, Emma. I never realized quite how much."

She smiled up into his eyes. "Come on, it *does* look like something from a fairy tale. It's positively enchanting."

The lights popped off again. He wondered vaguely why they'd gone on. Usually the lights stayed off unless someone was in residence. He decided Mulligan must be testing them.

"Even the hardest of hearts would be moved by this kind of beauty," Emma went on.

He looked down at her in the darkness and realized his hard heart was moved, but not by the lights or the garden or the star-filled sky. Their movements slowed until finally they were standing still, locked in each other's arms, gazing into each other's eyes. He wanted to kiss her. He was fairly certain she wanted the same thing.

But he couldn't do it.

With some internal effort, he pulled back. "Let's eat."

She looked disconcerted. *"Now?"*

He gave a quick nod and tried to dismiss the

tempting thoughts of her lips, her mouth, her body. "I'm starving," he said, with feeling.

The mood deflated like a popped balloon.

Emma sighed. "Okay, sure. Just give me a moment to get the cuttings and we can go." She started back toward the hill where they had been digging earlier.

Brice stood still for a moment, watching her go. He wanted to go after her, stop her, to pull her back into his arms and keep her there. But it wouldn't be fair to her. None of this was fair to her. And, damn it, it wasn't fair to him either. It was just the way it was.

He took a moment to collect himself, then followed her toward the hill.

Dinner was delicious, if uneventful. Emma spent virtually the whole time wondering what was going on with John that made him get close to her then pull back the way he did. If he never got close at all, she could understand it. After all, she was used to that sort of reaction from men. But he *had* kissed her, she was almost sure he had desired her. She might not be Miss Self-Esteem, but she knew when a man was looking at her as more than a friend, and John looked at her that way sometimes.

At least, she *thought* he did. She had to acknowledge that it could, possibly, just be wishful thinking on her part. She knew she was starting to look at him with more than mere platonic interest, despite the fact that alarms were going off in her heart. His friendship was important to her, she didn't want to risk losing it. Ever. Yet she was drawn to him physically, in a way she had never been drawn to any man before.

Theoretically, her twin feelings for John would have made for a perfect union. But that was only taking her own feelings into the equation. His feelings mattered too, and, while she couldn't figure out exactly what his feelings were, it was clear that he was pulling away from her. Perhaps he just wanted to be friends and keep it at that.

But, darn it, she'd spent a lifetime understanding when men just wanted to be friends with her. She'd spent years being the pal, the shoulder to cry on. This man was as close as she'd ever come to believing in a soul mate and *he'd kissed her*. He *must* be feeling the attraction she felt.

Mustn't he?

They got back to the room close to midnight. It seemed to Emma that John had pursued every idea *except* returning to the room, until finally they'd done everything there was to do in the sleepy town.

When they got to the room Emma slipped into the bathroom to change her clothes. All she had in the way of sleep clothes was a very long Mickey Mouse nightshirt. If she'd known they'd be sharing a room she would have at least brought some cotton pajamas or something a little more modest.

When she came out, John had changed into a T-shirt and soft cotton shorts. It was the most casual attire he'd appeared in since she'd met him. It suited him.

''I'm just putting together a sort of bed here on

the floor," he said when he saw her. "I took one of your pillows."

"Sleep on the bed, John. I don't mind sleeping on the floor," she said, hoping he would take the offer of the bed but refuse to let her take the floor.

"You're not going to sleep on the floor," he said, tossing two blankets and the pillow down. She tightened her jaw in anticipation, but all he said was, "I'm fine down here. Honestly."

"No, you're not," she insisted. "This is so stupid. Why don't we both just sleep on the bed? It's big enough." She gestured across the bed in illustration. It was just barely big enough for two.

John kept his eyes on the floor, busying himself with his makeshift bed. "This is fine, honestly, Emma." He bent down again, and the muscles of his legs flexed powerfully. What he wore was no different than what any other man might wear on a summer day, but somehow on John it was almost unbearably sexy.

As Emma got into bed she tried to keep her eyes—and her mind—off the sinewy length of muscle in his legs and shoulders as he shifted his weight. She cast thoughts of the rest of him from her mind, but the thoughts swung right back at her like a boomerang, time and again.

"Go on to sleep," he said, without turning around.

Emma shook her head. He was making himself very clear. She had to forget all romantic ideas about him and stick to the friendship they had forged so strongly for two years. Obviously that was what he wanted. Good lord, he wouldn't even look at her.

Maybe that was best, come to think of it. From the way her heart was pounding, her cheeks were probably flushed.

"All right, if you insist," she said, feeling rejected. "But if you're worried that I'll get the wrong idea if we sleep together in the bed, you're way off base."

He turned penetrating green eyes on her. "What would the wrong idea be, Emma?" he asked, with a small smile tugging at the corner of his mouth.

Her heart lurched. "Nothing...I—I just meant it would be a *practical* solution for two good friends...." Her voice was soft, barely audible, but he heard her.

They looked at each other for a long moment, neither of them speaking. Finally, he said, "The floor *doesn't* hold a lot of appeal, I must admit."

"Come on." She got out of bed and took a blanket from the floor, rolled it into a long cylinder, and placed it down the center of the bed. "There. My side and your side." She suddenly felt as though she were in a 1930s screwball-comedy movie.

He looked at her seriously. "I'd never want to hurt you, Emma."

The comment was so unexpected that she knew she looked comically surprised. "Hurt me? How? What do you mean?"

After a moment, he simply shook his head. "I only mean that I have a lot of respect for you. I would never try and take advantage of your trust." He looked pained. "Remember that, would you? No matter what happens."

"Of course. Gosh, are you going before a firing squad in the morning or something?"

He smiled. "No, I was just thinking how glad I am to have met you." He reached over and picked up the cylinder of blanket she'd just placed on the bed. "Mind if I remove this ridiculous thing?" he asked, amusement in his eyes.

"Go right ahead," she said, a little breathlessly.

"The bed is small enough with two people, this just takes up more room," he said, perhaps over-explaining.

"Yes, I see what you mean," she agreed.

She felt his eyes graze over her. Suddenly the long Mickey Mouse T-shirt felt revealing. She climbed back into the bed. It was an effort to seem casual, and she doubted that she was fooling him. Nevertheless, once in, she pulled the covers over her, rolled onto her side and said, "Good night."

"Good night." His voice was soft.

The light snapped off, and the bed creaked as he sat down. Emma practically had to hold on to the outer edge to keep from rolling into him. When he lay down, she felt the brush of his skin touch hers; legs touched legs, his arm pressed against her spine.

She was never going to get to sleep.

So she lay next to him, feeling the heat from his body, and looked out the window, trying to think of things other than the heat of his body. The moon was directly in the center of the pane, and Emma could see the water churning in the distance. Reflections of light danced upon it. They lay for a long time in silence. The bells of the church across the street rang midnight, then the half hour.

Emma rolled onto her back and stared at the ceiling in the dim room. Her bare leg was flush against his, and she could feel every hair on his against her skin. The heat between them increased. It was difficult not to reach her hand out to him. She counted the exposed beams several times, then finally whispered, "John? Are you awake?"

He answered immediately. "Yes."

She was suddenly very shy. "I hope *I* didn't wake you."

He gave a spike of laughter. "Not exactly."

"Well, I was just wondering…"

"What?"

She searched frantically for something reasonable to say. "I was wondering when you wanted to go back to London." She adjusted the sheet over her and put her arm down at her side. Her fingers touched his and remained.

He was still for a moment, then closed her hand in his. "Whenever you want."

A light wind blew in through the open window, raising the curtains. She could smell the very light spicy scent of his aftershave. "I could stay here forever," she said, edging toward him a fraction of an inch.

He turned to face her. "In some ways, I could, too." He touched her chin, then her cheek.

A wave of heat coursed down her body and settled in her pelvis. She turned her head. He was visible even in the near-dark. His eyes were trained on her, his beautiful mouth only inches from her own. "I..." Her voice trailed off. She couldn't find the words for what she was feeling.

John moved toward her and hovered, just for a moment, with his lips almost touching hers. Their breath mingled between them, and Emma found herself trembling. Finally, when she thought she might go mad with longing, he closed his mouth over hers.

Never in her life had Emma felt such a tidal wave of desire within herself. They moved their lips together, tongues touching, deliciously intermingled, then not at all. The kiss went from hungry, to gentle, to hungry again. For long moments, they lingered, still, lips barely touching. His scent was stronger up close; heady and delicious. Emma lifted a hand to his smooth cheek and ran her fingertips across the exquisite contours of his face. She wanted to speak, but words failed her.

He ran his hand down her back. The tickle caused her to arch toward him and her pelvis pressed against his arousal. He wanted her. The feel of him, pressed against her, increased her own ardor.

She slipped a leg between his and anchored them even closer together. His arms tightened around her, and he trailed kisses along her jaw and down to her shoulder. Then he stopped, holding her silently.

"I want to make love, John," Emma said, surprised by her bluntness.

His entire body stiffened for a moment, then his voice came, tense, "I do, too, believe me. But at the moment I don't think it's a good idea."

"No?" She couldn't help but sound hurt. "Is there

something…wrong?" A thousand physical explanations rushed through her mind.

He moved away and looked at her in the dark. "No, there's nothing wrong. I'm just trying to do the right thing for once."

"Your timing is perfect."

He turned onto his back and she studied his profile. A muscle clenched in his jaw. "I can't explain right now." He let out a ragged breath. "I will, soon, I swear it. After that…" He stopped, giving no further clue as to what on earth he was talking about.

Emma closed her eyes tightly. Silence followed. The church bells tolled the hour, cutting through the silence and through Emma's thoughts. Gradually it began to sound like a dirge in her mind, accompanying her dismal but inevitable thoughts. She now knew that he desired her. She knew he was attracted to her, at least a little, yet he said he had to do *the right thing*. He couldn't explain now, but he would soon.

What did it all mean?

Emma stared out the window for what seemed like hours but was probably twenty minutes. The moon had crossed to another part of the sky now, and all she could see was the steel gray of low-moving clouds. It suddenly felt ominous to her.

Her mind raced, trying to capture a comfortable explanation for John's behavior. Yet no matter where her thoughts veered, they always returned to one horrible conclusion.

There was another woman.

That had to be it. He was involved with someone

Play TIC-TAC-TOE and get FREE GIFTS!

HOW TO PLAY:

1. Play the tic-tac-toe scratch-off game at the right for your FREE BOOKS and FREE GIFT!

2. Send back this card and you'll receive TWO brand-new Silhouette Romance® novels. These books have a cover price of $3.50 each in the U.S. and $3.99 each in Canada, but they are yours to keep absolutely free.

3. There's no catch. You're under no obligation to buy anything. We charge nothing — ZERO — for your first shipment. And you don't have to make any minimum number of purchases — not even one!

4. The fact is, thousands of readers enjoy receiving books by mail from the Silhouette Reader Service™ months before they're available in stores. They like the convenience of home delivery, and they love our discount prices!

5. We hope that after receiving your free books you'll want to remain a subscriber. But the choice is yours — to continue or cancel, any time at all! So why not take us up on our invitation, with no risk of any kind. You'll be glad you did!

YOURS **FREE**
A FABULOUS **MYSTERY GIFT!**

We can't tell you what it is...
but we're sure you'll like it!

A FREE GIFT —
just for playing
TIC-TAC-TOE!

With a coin, scratch the gold boxes on the tic-tac-toe board. Then remove the "X" sticker from the front and affix it so that you get three X's in a row. This means you can get TWO FREE Silhouette Romance® novels and a **FREE MYSTERY GIFT!**

PLAY TIC-TAC-TOE

YES! Please send me the 2 Free books and gift for which I qualify. I understand that I am under no obligation to purchase any books, as explained on the back of this card.

315 SDL CX7T   **215 SDL CX7M**

(S-R-12/99)

Name:	
	(PLEASE PRINT CLEARLY)
Address:	Apt.#:
City:	State/Prov.:	Zip/Postal Code:

Offer limited to one per household and not valid to current Silhouette Romance® subscribers. All orders subject to approval.

PRINTED IN U.S.

The Silhouette Reader Service™ — Here's how it works:

Accepting your 2 free books and gift places you under no obligation to buy anything. You may keep the books and gift and return the shipping statement marked "cancel." If you do not cancel, about a month later we'll send you 6 additional novels and bill you just $2.90 each in the U.S., or $3.25 each in Canada, plus 25¢ delivery per book and applicable taxes if any.* That's the complete price and — compared to the cover price of $3.50 in the U.S. and $3.99 in Canada — it's quite a bargain! You may cancel at any time, but if you choose to continue, every month we'll send you 6 more books, which you may either purchase at the discount price or return to us and cancel your subscription.

*Terms and prices subject to change without notice. Sales tax applicable in N.Y. Canadian residents will be charged applicable provincial taxes and GST.

If offer card is missing write to: Silhouette Reader Service, 3010 Walden Ave., P.O. Box 1867, Buffalo, NY 14240-1867

BUSINESS REPLY MAIL
FIRST-CLASS MAIL   PERMIT NO. 717   BUFFALO, NY

POSTAGE WILL BE PAID BY ADDRESSEE

SILHOUETTE READER SERVICE
3010 WALDEN AVE
PO BOX 1867
BUFFALO NY 14240-9952

NO POSTAGE
NECESSARY
IF MAILED
IN THE
UNITED STATES

else but had never bothered to tell Emma because their relationship was, in some ways, beyond that kind of thing. Talking about someone else would have been so irrelevant, though if he had she wouldn't have minded. Before she met him, that was, she wouldn't have minded at all.

But she'd never imagined that they'd have a romantic attraction to each other. Yet she did to him, and it was fairly safe to guess that he did to her, since he'd kissed her. And that kiss had changed everything.

They'd left the boundaries of friendship and gotten stuck in the mud of romantic attraction. Even if they could somehow sludge back to safer ground, they'd always have that little bit of dirt on their shoes…the memory of illicit kisses and longing that couldn't be satisfied. It would stand between them forever now.

The last thing she saw before finally falling asleep was that the clouds had broken again, and this time two little stars winked at her.

Chapter Six

The next day, Emma told John she wanted to go to a bookstore to try and find some books on the local environment and history. Because she wasn't sure when she would next be able to afford a trip to England, she wanted to have as much information about the area as possible for her research.

"I wish I could stay here," she said, as they walked into the middle of town. "I mean, apart from how beautiful it is, it would just be so much easier to do the research from here."

"Then stay," John said simply.

Her heart tripped. Did he want her to stay? Or was he just making the obvious suggestion after what she'd said? "The lab doesn't have the money to put me up here indefinitely and set up a local lab, and I certainly don't." She shrugged, but watched him closely. He gave no sign of what he was feeling.

"This whole thing is a crapshoot, really. If the cuttings survive the trip home, then I have to hope they'll take root in a new environment. It may not work at all."

John slowed his pace. "What if you could get some sort of, I don't know, sponsor or something? Someone who would fund a lab here. Then would you stay?"

"In a heartbeat." Maybe he *did* want her to stay. "But who would fund such an expensive and uncertain project? Truth is, it's a risky investment."

"With you in charge?" He cocked his head. "I doubt it's too big a risk."

A smile welled up inside her. "That's very nice of you, but unrealistic, I'm afraid."

"Still…given the chance, would you stay?"

She didn't hesitate. "Given the chance, I definitely would." She thought for a moment, then amended, "Probably."

He nodded and continued to look thoughtful as they walked.

"I'm sure the bookstore is right around here someplace," he said as they got into a square that was heavily populated with shoppers. "Let's try down there."

They turned and walked into a shaded alley. There was nothing there but a fancy restaurant and a shop called Gepetto. When she looked in the window, Emma saw that it was full of puppets.

"Oh, John, let's go in here, just for a minute."

He glanced up and saw what she was talking about. *"Puppets?"*

She smiled. "Just for a minute." Without waiting for the male objection she expected, she went into the store. It was so cluttered with puppets that she felt as though she was standing before a huge crowd of people. She picked up an intricate court jester marionette and examined it closely. The porcelain face had been painted in exacting detail, clearly by hand. The expression was the melancholy sadness that Emma usually associated with clowns. It looked nearly human, right down to the faint laugh lines by its emerald-green eyes. The medieval outfit was blue silk, with embroidered patterns of red and gold. In its small lifelike hand it held a mask, which could be raised to fit perfectly against the face. The mask was bright and colorful, the red mouth drawn up in an exaggerated smile.

Emma held the puppet for awhile, studying the features and fitting the mask on and off until John came up behind her. "What's that?"

She held it up for his perusal. "A two-faced clown." She held it up for him to see. "Isn't it amazing?"

He looked skeptical. "You really like this thing?"

"I feel sorry for it." She laughed, trying to lighten the strange weight of empathy she felt for the toy. "In a way I hate to put it back on the shelf."

John frowned, but there was a smile in his eyes. "You feel sorry for the puppet?"

She nodded. "Look at him. He's a clown, so everyone expects him to be happy. But he's not happy. So in order to be the clown that everyone wants him to be, he has to use a mask. No wonder he's sad." She sighed. "I've felt like that myself sometimes," she said, more to herself than to him.

John looked at her without speaking. His face was full of some emotion—trepidation, perhaps? Fear that Emma had gone off the deep end?

"On the other hand, maybe he's one of those puppets that likes being sad." She met the shopkeeper's gaze behind a wall of small faces and bodies, and gave an appreciative nod. His face opened into a delighted smile, and he nodded back and gestured for her to browse freely.

"Do you want it?" John asked her.

She made a face and whispered, "Look at the price."

He gave it a brief glance, and shrugged. "If you want it, I'll get it for you."

She raised an eyebrow, loving the fact that he treated her so gallantly but puzzled by the scope of his generosity. "I don't think you read that right. Or I didn't." She took the marionette and looked at the paper price tag. "Nope, I read it right. That is pounds, right? Not lire?"

The corner of his mouth tugged toward a smile. "Pounds."

She gave a low whistle. "How rich would you have to be to be able to afford that much for something like this? My used car cost less than that. Sorry, buddy, you have to go back." She set it back on the shelf, with a brief wave to the owner.

They went back out into the bright sunlight and found themselves in the midst of a crowd. "Everyone's up early today," John commented dryly. "I never realized this island could hold so many people."

Emma stopped. "You took those pictures in the spring, wasn't it busy then?"

He shrugged. "I guess I didn't notice it then."

"Well, I like it." They continued walking. "It reminds me of something. Wasn't there a painter who did a series of café paintings in a place like this? I studied them in college. The atmosphere was just like this." Everywhere she turned there was something picturesque. To the right, it was the couple huddled close at a small bistro table, his cigarette smoke wafting around them from the tin ashtray on the table. To the left, there was an expanse of green park with bushes cut into the shapes of animals.

And straight ahead there was a bookshop. "*There* it is," she said, pointing.

John looked in the direction she indicated. "Why don't you go ahead. I'll try and get a table at that bistro there. You meet me when you're finished."

There was already a crowd at the entrance to the bistro, but the patio tables were so quaint that Emma figured it would probably be worth waiting for. "You sure you don't mind waiting in line?"

"Not at all. Go." She hesitated and he said again, "Go on."

She went and quickly found several books on the local environment, including one on historic houses. She started to take them to the cash register, then, following an impulse she couldn't quite explain, she stopped and went to the garden and nature section. The British edition of John's book was displayed facing out, and she was drawn right to it. The cover looked basically the same as the one she had, but it was slightly larger and there were two other photos inserted in the bottom corners.

She picked up the book and leafed through. It was the same inside, though she still thought she should get it for a souvenir. She took it to the register and laid it facedown with the other books, then gasped. Unlike the American edition, the British one had a photo of the author on the back.

But the photo wasn't of John.

The man in the picture had a ruddy freckled complexion and light auburn hair. The brief biography below the picture was the same one she'd read a thousand times in her book. Only the man was different. Quite different. There was no mistaking the difference for a trick of the light or an old photo. He didn't look anything like the John Turnhill who was now waiting for her in the café outside.

Why?

Emma tried to catch her breath. This made no sense. Why would there be a photo of someone else instead of John? Someone wasn't being honest. Her mind raced. Who was the impostor? The guy in the picture or the guy in the café? How could it be the man she'd spent the last few days with? He knew everything about their correspondence over the past two years. He *had* to be the real John Turnhill. Didn't he?

In a suspended daze, Emma paid for the books and carried the bag back outside, into the too-bright sunshine.

Something was very, very wrong here and she had the nagging feeling that her John—the one she'd come with—wasn't quite who he said he was. In a strange way she wasn't entirely surprised. It was almost as if she'd known something was amiss ever since she'd met John, but she couldn't quite put her finger on it.

Well, she was going to put her finger on it now.

With greater purpose, she increased her strides, hurrying to the café where she could see John sitting at a table on the sidewalk. Something like relief warmed her chest when she saw him. There had to be an explanation. She trusted John as she'd never trusted anyone before. Surely her instincts weren't wrong about him.

But if they were, she thought, unease returning, she had to know it.

Brice wasn't absolutely sure that he was going to tell Emma who he really was. Last night, when they'd come so close to making love, he'd determined that he *would* tell her and let her react however she was going to react. There was a chance that she would accept it, perhaps it wouldn't even matter to her once the initial shock had passed, and their relationship could progress as they both seemed to want it to. He gave a bitter laugh. Who was he fooling? He was almost certain that once he told her she would leave and never come back. It would be the end of their friendship. He couldn't stand that. His thoughts returned to last night. Resisting Emma had been one of the most difficult things he had ever done in his life. In a way it all seemed senseless—she wanted him, he wanted her—why not follow the call of nature?

He knew the answer. Because it was wrong to involve her under false circumstances. She wanted to make love to John Turnhill, the photographer. A man who had come from ordinary beginnings to live a secure but quiet life in North London. He had no conglomerate to run, no title to uphold, no tradition to follow. John Turnhill was the sort of man Emma Lawrence could make a life with.

He looked up and saw her coming toward him, holding a large paper bag from the bookstore, and realized he was at a complete loss as to what to do.

"Did you find what you were looking for?" he asked, standing and pulling out her chair for her.

She stood before him, her face pale and her mouth set in a hard line. "And more," she said, taking out a copy of John Turnhill's book. She handed it to Brice. "Please tell me there's a simple explanation for this."

"I don't understand," he said, an unnamed dread growing in him. "Don't you have this already?"

"Not this one." She turned the book over in his hands.

John Turnhill's picture stared up at him.

He felt the blood drain from his face.

"Emma, I can explain this—"

Her shoulders relaxed fractionally. "I was hoping you would."

"Please," he said quietly. "Sit down." When she didn't move, he said again, "Please."

Without taking her eyes off him, she sat. "Okay, so what's going on here, John?"

Where could he begin? How could he possibly explain this so she'd understand and not hate him? Was that even possible? "Emma, there *is* a simple explanation for this, really—"

Before he could go on, an older couple stopped right behind Emma, wide-eyed and open-mouthed.

"I can't believe it," the older woman said, in a Wagnerian voice. "Brice? Brice, darling, whatever are you doing here?" *Brice*. He could see Emma turn and take in the woman, who was in her late sixties, wearing too much makeup and garbed from head to toe in heavy Chanel chains.

Brice felt a cold finger of apprehension trace down his spine. This was it. The end had come, the truth was barreling toward them like a train and there was nothing he could do to stop it.

He stood, took the woman's extended hand, and gave a stiff bow. "Good morning, Baroness Penman." He kissed the hand, then pivoted slightly and took the man's hand. "Baron."

The older man shook his hand, a pleasant expression on his face. "Good to see you, my boy. I say, this is something of a surprise. Your mother was recently lamenting the fact that you never come to Sheldale House anymore."

Brice felt Emma's eyes on him. "Is that so?"

"Oh, my, yes." The baroness's jowls shook with mirth. "But you know how your mother fancies the idea of the lord returning to the manor."

Brice felt Emma's gaze intensify. The awkwardness of the moment was overwhelming. He gestured toward her, and said, "This is my friend, Emma Lawrence, from America." He lowered himself back into his seat, aware that his life had taken a surreal turn and any moment now he was going to have to speak intelligently. "We were just having breakfast."

The couple acknowledged Emma with vague gestures and noises of how-do-you-do. Emma did the same.

There followed an uncomfortable silence, during which Brice did his best to casually sip his coffee. Anyone who looked at him would have seen his hand shake. He set the cup down with a loud clank.

"And how long are you in Guernsey, Brice?" The baroness asked. "Are you staying beyond the party tomorrow night?"

"Party?"

The older woman frowned. "Yes, at Sheldale House. Funny, your mother didn't mention you would be here...you're not planning on slipping away before then, are you?"

Brice shook his head, the blood thundering through his veins. His mother's annual Midsummer ball. She was having it at *Sheldale* this year? She always had it at her sprawling Lansworth estate in Sheffield—why the change this year of all years? He really ought to start reading her letters. No wonder the housekeeper had been so confused when he said he was coming but didn't want her to act as though she knew him. "No. No, I'm not," he said to the older couple, without offering further information.

The woman eyed him sternly and straightened her considerable form. "We'll be at the dinner beforehand as well. I understand it will be much more intimate this year. Caroline will be there, I assume." She flicked her gaze at Emma.

Caroline would be there? Brice couldn't have written himself into more of a spot if he'd tried. "Perhaps."

"My dear," her husband said gently, apparently picking up on the thick tension they'd walked into. "I believe we should be on our way now." He met Brice's eyes. "So much to do, you know. Hate to interrupt your breakfast."

Brice nodded, grateful for the man's sensitivity. He stood again. "Very good to see you again, sir." He turned to the baroness. "And you, Baroness."

She gave him a quick peck on the cheek and turned to go without acknowledging Emma again. The baron, however, did give her a nod and a small smile before turning to follow his wife.

When they were gone, Brice searched for the words, but nothing came to him. He was numb.

Well, the question of whether to tell or not was answered, he thought, trying to put order to the confusion in his mind. Truth prevailed once again. She would hate him for his lies, if not his identity, but at least she would know the truth. There was some relief in that. Keeping up the pretense had been tremendously taxing.

So in that sense this was good.

But in virtually every other sense it was bad. Really, really bad.

It was Emma who broke the silence. "*What* was that all about?"

He turned to her. Could he stall the inevitable? "You mean the baron and baroness?"

"Yes."

"Delightful people."

"Charming."

"I don't think I've seen them since…"

"Stop it!" Emma's face flushed pink. "Are you going to tell me what's happening here or not? Why did they call you Brice?"

He took a long sip of hot coffee, welcoming the burn down his throat. He reached for her hand. How could he say it? *I've been lying to you for two years.* "I am not exactly who you think I am."

Her face had grown pale and drawn. "That is becoming frighteningly clear. Please tell me what this is about. What's this about a party at Sheldale House and your mother?"

He sighed heavily and then just said it. "I'm not John Turnhill."

She looked as though she might be sick. "You're…not John?"

"I never was," he said quickly. Then, realizing how idiotic that sounded, he amended, "I'm the man you've been writing to, and who's been writing to you, it's just the name that's not the same."

She shook her head and made a weak gesture with her hand. "Elaborate."

This wasn't as easy to explain as he would have thought. "I'm John Turnhill, that's just not my name."

She stared at him for a moment, then gave a single nod. "Then what's your name?"

"My name," he took a deep breath and forced the words out, "is Brice, the earl of Palliser."

Chapter Seven

She jerked her hand away from his and shook her head. "What do you mean you're Brice Palliser? You can't be! That's ridiculous."

"I am." When, in the past, he'd entertained the idea of making this admission, he'd never dreamed he'd actually have to work to get her to believe him. Yet it beat the slap in the face and the hasty exit he *had* expected. "You see, when you wrote to John Turnhill about the St. Paul's Heart, he passed the letter along to me and I wrote back and before you knew it—"

He could see her trying to grasp the concept. "You can't just get letters under a fake name and fake address for two years," she protested. "I don't believe this."

Brice hesitated. What could he do next? He'd finally told the truth and she didn't believe him. It was remarkable. For a fleeting moment, he wondered if he could keep up the pretense of being John Turnhill, now that he had given a good, honest try at telling her the truth.

But he wouldn't knowingly take advantage of Emma on a technicality, no matter how much he wanted to salvage things. "Emma, I'm telling you the truth. John's a friend of mine. He set your letters aside for me and I picked them up when they arrived."

She was obviously growing more upset. "When did I stop writing to him and start writing to you?"

"You've always written to me. When you originally wrote to John Turnhill, he didn't know the answer to your question about the St. Paul's Heart, so, as I said, he handed it off to me. It seemed harmless enough to answer for him, and in his name, because he was the author of the book and the man you had written to. As I said, I didn't know we would continue writing. By the time I realized it, it was too late for me to say, 'Incidentally, I'm not who you think I am.'"

"So I've been writing to an earl," she said dully.

"Yes."

"And you probably have, maybe, a hundred lesser titles too, right?" Her tone was flat, as though every title drove the wedge further between them. "And a seat in the House of Lords."

He answered perfunctorily. "I have nine other titles and I rarely go to the House of Lords."

"But you can." She shot it like an accusation.

"Yes, I can," he conceded, then looked her straight in the eye. "Does that make a difference?"

"Does it make a *difference?* You're not who I thought you were *at all.*" Her voice rose. "As a matter of fact, you couldn't be *more* different from who I thought you were unless you were the queen herself."

"No, Emma, you're wrong." This was so much harder than he'd thought it would be. He realized, all at once, that the reserve John had called coldness was actually something he'd used all his life to avoid having to face and justify his emotions. His instinct, even now, was to slip behind the safety of it. But for the first time in his life he knew that if he closed that door once more, it might never open again. "I'm exactly who you think I am. Emma," he touched her cheek, "I was more myself with you than I've ever been with anyone in my life."

A long moment passed, then she looked at him and said, "You lied to me."

His chest constricted painfully. "I never meant to. Circumstances just spun out of control. Surely you can see how that could happen."

For just a moment her expression softened, then she narrowed her eyes. "One letter I can understand. Maybe two." Emma grimaced. "But after that..." She shook her head. "Why would you keep the pretense up for two entire years?"

He didn't answer immediately. He sighed, letting the breath drain from his lungs. "Because I liked not being Brice Palliser. When I was John, you accepted me for what I *was,* not for what you thought I *should* be. I was a faceless stranger who you liked for no other reason than himself.''

"That wouldn't have changed if you'd used your real name. What difference would it have made? A man is made by character, not by his name, rank or position."

"Usually." Brice gave a resigned nod. "That's the sort of thing most people can take for granted. For me, it's never been the case. People tend to either bow and scrape or they resent the hell out of me. There's nothing in between. Come on, Emma, would you *really* have continued writing to the earl of Palliser? Would you really have felt as comfortable with our correspondence under those circumstances?''

She looked at the photo on the book. "Maybe not," she admitted at last. "But we'll never know for sure." She lowered her head into her hands. "I feel like such a fool."

"No, Emma, *I'm* the fool. I should have found a way to tell you the truth long ago. It was just…too difficult." He reached out to touch her arm but she recoiled.

"You're right." She looked at him and both her gaze and her voice became chilly. "You should have done it anyway."

He didn't know what to say to that. He couldn't argue, but neither could he grovel and beg for forgiveness. Neither of them was the type for that kind of scene. "Yes, I should have," he said at last, then shrugged weakly. "I'm sorry."

She stood up. "I've got to go."

"Where?" He started to stand, but she held up a hand to stop him.

"I need to be alone for awhile. I need to think, to let this sink in."

He clenched his jaw and nodded. "I understand."

She glanced at her watch and started, "I'll meet—" With a brusque shake of her head, she stopped. He knew, even though she hadn't finished, that she had been on the verge of arranging to meet him later, but she'd caught herself. Responsibility was a hard habit to break, but this betrayal was too big to brush aside. "I'm going now," she said, and turned to leave.

He watched her go with a profound sense of lost opportunity. There were so many doors that could open now that he'd told the truth, if only she would turn the single key of forgiveness: he could finance a lab for her, he could let her stay on either at Sheldale House or in his London home, they could see each other whenever they wanted without the end of her vacation looming overhead.

They could even move forward with the romantic attraction they both clearly had felt.

Yet he had the doomed feeling that she wouldn't turn the key. Good intentions aside, he'd betrayed her, and he knew it. If he were to bring up how things could be now, it would look as if he was trying to buy her forgiveness and that would be decidedly unforgivable. Things were out of his control. He'd just have to wait and see what happened.

Emma walked along the water's edge and tried to make sense of the thoughts that crowded her mind.

John was Brice. There was no John. The friend she'd valued so much for so long didn't exist at all. Or, to the degree that he did exist, he was a hologram. The ironic thought came to her that as a child, she'd never had an imaginary friend. She'd certainly never dreamed she'd have one in her twenties.

She started to laugh but the knot of emotion in her chest forced its way into her throat and she had to fight back tears. There was no John. No simple little gingerbread-style house on Cecile Park Road in North London. She'd addressed her last letter there before she'd gotten on the plane, happily oblivious to the upheaval she was about to face. It was almost as if he'd died.

John was the earl of Palliser. And nine other equally unreachable titles.

It was unthinkable. The earl she'd pictured was a foppish old man, walking about his estate with a bowler hat and walking stick. In reality, the earl was a young and vibrant man, a man as handsome as a movie star...just as fanciful girls pictured Prince Charming. And he was, for a short time and in a strange way, hers.

John was Brice Palliser.

He'd always been Brice Palliser. She stopped and sat down on the shore, slipping off her sandals and dipping her toes in the cool water. He'd *always* been Brice Palliser. She let that thought sink in for several minutes. In that sense, nothing had changed. Only the name.

Was that really such a huge betrayal? Or was it,

as he'd said, an innocent circumstance that had spun way out of control? Granted, after what had happened at work, she'd spent years trying to learn to trust people again, to take them at face value and not constantly look beneath the surface with suspicion. And John—that is, Brice—knew that. But what had happened at work was a different situation—it had been a frame-up, with reckless disregard for her reputation and even her freedom. The person who had done that to her had done it methodically and with malicious intent.

She *knew* Brice hadn't had any malicious intent. In fact, she was a little surprised to realize—when she examined her feelings—that she didn't feel all that *hurt* from his revelation. It was mostly disappointment, sadness about the schoolgirl fantasies she'd had of life with him. They weren't his fault. He hadn't set out to make her feel anything at all about him. Yes, he'd lied, but he'd had what he felt were compelling reasons for it.

She tried to imagine herself in his place. She could understand writing the first letter in John Turnhill's name, she really could. And the second, too, now that she thought of it. That second letter she'd written was to inquire about the woods behind the St. Paul's Heart, how deep the shade was in the summer, things like that. But she'd made some droll comment about Robin Hood and he'd written back, elaborating the point. From there it had become a running joke and a running correspondence.

Had she been in his place, could she have interrupted the flow of written conversation to say *by the way, that's not my real name?* And if she'd been a wealthy, titled aristocrat, *would* she have made such an admission to a stranger across the ocean, even if she had a nice rapport with him in writing?

She honestly wasn't sure.

He'd said he'd been more himself with her in their letters than he had ever been in his real life. She could see that, now that she reflected on the days they'd spent together. There was a reserve about him that she recognized as a quality in someone who always feels responsible for what's going on around him. It wasn't a control issue, precisely, it was more a kind of accountability. It made perfect sense, considering the responsibilities he bore—an earl with nine lesser titles, three major estates, and a seat in the House of Lords; the head of one of the oldest families in Britain; the president of an international technology corporation...it was a lot for one man to take on. It wore on him, too, she could see that.

No wonder he'd enjoyed relinquishing that in his letters. She wasn't the only one who'd lost something here. In fact, she hadn't really lost that much—John had always been Brice. But Brice, for his part, could never be John again. Who was she to begrudge him that single pleasure? Especially since he hadn't really done her any harm.

A boat crossed her line of vision on the sea before her, soothing her with its slowly rocking motion. She relaxed and took a breath. This vacation had changed her, even before Brice had told her who he really was. He'd made her feel attractive, witty, desired. He'd made her days romantic and exciting; every morning that she woke up under these foreign skies, she'd felt as if an adventure awaited her with John. Moreover, he'd nurtured her dream to study the St. Paul's Heart and be the one to make the breakthrough discovery of its miraculous properties. She couldn't remember ever feeling so strong, so full of purpose. *He'd* done all of that for her. It had nothing to do with what he called himself, or what she called him, it was the man inside who had touched the woman inside of her.

She leaned back and closed her eyes, reliving the memories of the past few days. Warm memories made her smile. Things fell into place now, like why he'd seemed distracted, and why he hadn't always answered her when she spoke his name. She laughed ironically. It must have been very hard for him to keep up the pretense and to remember who he was.

Her thoughts drifted to last night. Lying by his side in the dark, kissing him, wanting so much more. *I want to make love, John,* Emma had said.

I do, too, believe me. But at the moment I don't think it's a good idea.

Is there something wrong? she'd asked him.

What had he said to that? She frowned and tried to remember. It was significant now, she knew it.

Then it came to her.

I'm just trying to do the right thing for once, he'd said. *I can't explain right now. I will, soon, I swear it. After that...*

After that, what? Her chest tightened and a tingle tripped down the back of her neck. He'd wanted her. They'd felt the same thing last night, but his honor had kept him from taking advantage of her while she didn't know exactly what was going on. There weren't a lot of men like that.

And he was an *earl*. For the first time, the thought made her smile. Wow. The earl of Palliser. What was the wife of an earl called? she wondered crazily. A countess? Countess Emma Palliser. Her face grew warm but her heart tripped giddily. She was being as silly as a schoolgirl. Americans didn't marry into families like that. Did they? Could they? Could an ordinary American girl really date an English lord? Suddenly she had to find out.

And she was wasting time, sitting here mulling it all over. When she'd left Brice she'd been in a snit. She had to get back to him, and fast, to tell him she didn't hate him. To tell him she understood why he'd done what he had, and that she knew it wasn't really a betrayal to her.

Most important, she had to find out where their relationship stood, now that she knew the truth.

An hour later, Emma stood in front of the café where she'd left Brice. He wasn't there. Panic niggled in her chest. She'd been so sure he'd be there, where she'd left him. Where had he gone? Could he have left the island, believing that she wanted nothing more to do with him?

No, that was crazy thinking. It was panic talking, not reason. She hadn't been gone long enough for him to do anything drastic. But she had to find him before he did draw the wrong conclusions and feel awful. She thought frantically. Where could he have gone?

It occurred to her that he might have gone to Sheldale House, but if she went there to look and ran into a member of the staff—or even his mother, who was evidently in town—her explanation for being on the private property might seem flimsy. No, she'd wait until she'd exhausted all other possibilities first.

She decided she'd start with the hotel. The fifteen-minute walk seemed interminable, even though she ran at least half of it. When she got to the door she was breathless. Taking just a moment to collect herself, so she wouldn't look completely ridiculous, she opened the door.

He was there. Thank goodness.

But he was packing his bag.

"You're leaving?" Emma said, in a questioning tone. She'd been right. Her instincts had told her he'd draw the wrong conclusion and think he was doing the best thing for her by getting away from her, and now it looked as if she'd been correct.

He stopped and turned to her. "I wasn't going to just slip out like a thief, no." He gestured toward the desk. "I wrote a note."

She didn't move. "What does it say?"

He kept his gaze even on her. "It says how sorry I am to have disappointed you, but that I understand what a shock this is and how you undoubtedly need time to come to terms with it. It says that I'll be at the Sheldale House for another couple of days and after that, I'll be in London and you can contact me there if you'd like."

She took a short breath. "Does it say what you want me to do?"

He hesitated, then shook his head, still holding her gaze. "At the moment, I don't have the right to want you to do anything for my sake."

"Our desires don't always agree with our rights."

"I find they almost never do."

"Brice." She swallowed. "The other night, when you said there was something you had to explain before we could…" She couldn't put it to words, so she let her voice trail off and gave a weak smile. "Was this what you meant? Or do you have some other deep, dark secret on top of this?"

He laughed quietly, and met her eyes. "This was it."

"You're not also…I don't know…" she smiled, "the heir to the throne or something."

"No. Just the earl of Palliser."

"Well, that's enough," she said tentatively. "It changes things a little between us."

"I understand."

She took a breath. "I mean, you'll have to give me your real address, for one thing."

He looked at her. "I'm sorry?"

"You'll have to give me your real address. I can't keep writing to John Turnhill now, can I? I mean, really, *that* would be ludicrous."

"Keep writing?"

She nodded.

"Are you saying you've accepted this? That we're…all right?"

She chose her words carefully. "I'm surprised. Of

course.'' She smiled. "I'm a little disappointed that you didn't find some way to break it to me *before* I spent days calling you 'John' to your face. But...I don't want to lose you, particularly over a situation that could almost certainly never be repeated.''

He smiled and moved in front of her. "You're not going to rethink this in a little while and say you've changed your mind, are you?''

She shook her head. "I only have a few days left here. I don't want to waste them playing games.''

He cupped her face with his hands and bent down to kiss her, quickly, on the lips. "Pack your things. We're getting out of here.''

"What do you mean?''

"I mean, if we have a couple more days together we shouldn't spend them in this hotel.''

"Why not?''

"Because we don't have to be cramped up in here like this now.''

The space hadn't seemed all that cramped to Emma but she knew she and Brice had different perspectives about living conditions. "Where do you want to go?''

"Anywhere you want. Why not Sheldale?''

She felt her face light up as a mental picture of herself staying in a grand English country home came to her. "*Really?* We can go stay there?''

He nodded. "Unless you're uncomfortable with that.''

She lowered her chin and looked at him. "Of course it's not my usual standard, but I'll try to get used to it.''

"Do."

"This will be *amazing*." She went to the dresser and started pulling her clothes out and tossing them onto the bed. "I've always wondered what it was like to stay in a place like that. I've seen them advertised for rent and as hotels and things, but they were always far out of my price range."

"I hope you're not disappointed."

"No way." She pushed the drawer shut. "What about this party your mother's having there?" She felt him freeze behind her.

"That's right, I forgot about it. Did you want to go to that?" Immediately he added, "No, that's a bad idea."

She turned to face him. "Why? Don't you want to go?"

It was as though a wall went up between them. Suddenly, Brice was a younger version of the staid old earl she'd envisioned. "Those functions aren't really all that interesting. You'd probably have a much better time if we went back to London."

"Really? It seems like it would be a kick to go to a party at one of the great houses of Britain."

His gaze was penetrating. "It's not like you'd imagine. Remember the baron and baroness?"

Emma nodded.

He was clearly resistant to the idea. "There will be hundreds of people just like them there."

"Real characters, huh?"

He shrugged, but there was a tension inside the gesture that told her he wasn't nearly as blasé about it as he appeared. "Really dull characters."

A cold feeling came over her. "Wait a minute, is this about me not liking them or about me not fitting in with them?"

He hesitated and when he spoke, the answer didn't come quickly enough to reassure her. "This kind of function is always a competition of power and wealth. It's boring at best and ugly at worst. I wouldn't want to subject you to that."

He was embarrassed to take her. She knew it. Her heart fell, but what could she do? There was nothing to argue about. If he didn't want to take her to meet his family and friends, bickering about it wouldn't help. She took a breath and tried to sound cheerful, but failed. "Look," she hauled her suitcase to the bed and began putting things in it, "why don't we just go back to London then? I've finished everything I need to do at Sheldale House right now anyway."

He wasn't fooled for a minute. "Emma, I'm not worried that you won't fit in. You're the most charming woman I've ever known. Honestly."

It was difficult to meet his eyes but she forced herself to. She'd always been impatient with the kind of girls who sulked. "It's okay," she said, picking up a pair of socks. "I don't have anything to wear to something like that anyway."

He let out a long, ragged breath. "There's a shop in town where you could get something."

She let the words sink in before looking up at him, still clutching the socks. "Are you saying you want to go to the party after all?"

He shook his head. "I can't say I want to *go* exactly. But I want to take you. Maybe I'm being self-

ish, because I know this won't be as much fun as
you imagine, but I want to introduce you to the people in my life.''

Her heart filled like a helium balloon and she
thought she just might drift up to the ceiling. ''Really? Do you mean it?''

''I mean it.'' He went to her and took the socks
out of her hand. ''We'd better go now if you hope
to have something chosen and altered by tomorrow
evening.''

Altered? She'd never had to buy something and
have it tailored before. Emma was strictly an off-the-
rack kind of girl. But as she looked at the regal man
standing before her—the *earl of Palliser*, for Pete's
sake—she got the first real inkling that none of her
existing ways of doing things were going to work in
his world.

Chapter Eight

Late that afternoon, Brice and Emma went back to Sheldale House, this time with their bags and their intentions to stay for a few days. He had a bad feeling about it. It had been one thing to walk the grounds at twilight with the belief that no one would be around to interact with them. It was quite another to come to the front courtyard knowing that his approach was anticipated and would bring with it a certain amount of fanfare. The role of prodigal son returning was not one that Brice particularly relished. But the wheels were already in motion and there was no stopping them. If he insisted they leave the island, Emma would draw the quiet conclusion that he was ashamed of her and he couldn't bear that.

The door opened as they walked up the brick steps and Leila Moran, the head housekeeper for as long as Brice could remember, curtsied and said, "Welcome back, Lord Palliser. We're honored to have you."

"Leila." He gave a curt nod and ushered Emma in, past a veritable receiving line of staff who bowed and curtsied as he passed, almost certainly making Emma uncomfortable.

"Brice, darling," his mother's familiar voice rang from down the hall.

He cringed inside. If Emma wasn't already uncomfortable, she was about to be. He only hoped his mother didn't mention Caroline before he had the chance to explain her to Emma first. He'd begun to three or four times already, but every time he started, he heard his own words and realized what a deceitful person he was sounding like. He wanted at least a small chance to be with Emma as himself—to let her trust him for himself—before springing another thing on her.

His mother appeared a moment later, fashionably dressed in a gray silk pantsuit that emphasized her too-thin form. She held both her hands out to him as she approached. "I'm so glad you've decided to join us this year."

"Mother." He took her hands and kissed both cheeks before stepping back and saying, "Mother, I'd like you to meet a friend of mine. This is Emma Lawrence, from America. Emma, my mother, Lillian Palliser, Lady Sorrelsby."

"Please, call me Lillian." Lillian Palliser extended a hand to Emma. "So very pleased to meet you, my dear. I must admit, I was quite surprised when Brice telephoned and said he'd be coming and bringing an

American friend. Tell me, what part of the States are you from?''

It would have been difficult for the average person to tell that Emma was nervous, but Brice realized it immediately by the seconds' hesitation before she spoke. "In Maryland, near Washington, D.C."

Lillian clapped her hands together. "Lovely city. I've been there many times. Brice's late father had a cousin in congress, and my dear friend Marlene worked in the embassy there in early 1996. She'll be here tomorrow, in fact. You must catch us all up on the gossip there.''

Emma smiled. "I'm not sure I have any interesting gossip to share. I don't think we know the same people.''

Brice saw his mother's smile drop a notch. "Well, then, you can tell us about something else.''

Brice interjected. "I told Leila to prepare the blue room near mine for Emma.'' He glanced at the housekeeper. "Would you take her bags, please?''

The woman nodded and, with a quick glance at his mother, perhaps waiting for an objection, lifted the bags and took them up the long, curved stairway.

Lillian watched as Leila carried the beat-up duffle bag to the second floor. "My dear, where is your ball gown for tomorrow night?''

Emma colored. "We stopped on the way here—''

"It's at the tailor's,'' Brice said easily. He knew his mother didn't mean to make Emma uncomfortable, but it came naturally to her, nevertheless. "Really, mother, you mustn't worry so about everyone else.'' He took Emma's arm. "We're going out to the lawn for tea." He glanced at a maid, who still stood by the front door, watching them. "See to it, would you, Christina?"

"Yes, sir." She curtsied and hurried off toward the kitchens.

He walked Emma toward the back of the house, his own tension rising. "I hope you don't regret checking out of the hotel. This place can be quite cold at night." It was a lame attempt to get her interested in leaving, but he gave it a try anyway. He knew she'd find the party anticlimactic.

"It's incredible here," Emma said, slowing her pace to look in the library as they passed. "Good heavens, there must be a million books in there."

"Emma," he began.

"Yes?" She looked at him with large, innocent eyes.

He sighed heavily then took her by the arm and swept her into the library. It might be the only opportunity they'd get for privacy until they left. He closed the door behind them. "Emma, are you absolutely sure you want to stay and go through with this?"

She looked bemused. "Why? What's wrong?"

"Nothing's *wrong* precisely, I just think you'd enjoy yourself more if we went somewhere else..." How could he explain? He was afraid she would be thoroughly disillusioned with him when she realized how staid his life was. And even if she wasn't, if she didn't get enough of a taste to see what it was really like, it wasn't as though he could marry her and let her in for it. He thought about the Emma he'd grown to know in her letters, the things that gave her pleasure, the things that made her crazy. She loved "playing in the mud," as she called it, working in the garden in her old jeans and the battered straw hat that had been her grandmother's. He had a picture of her in it somewhere. She hated getting dressed up in what she called "grown-up clothes" and going to meetings and symposiums like the one she'd gone to in London this week. She loved to set her own schedule and work by herself on her studies, taking however much time they needed to grow under her nurturing touch. She hated to fit her life around other peoples' schedules and work at a pace designated by someone else.

But life with Brice would be full of those things she hated—charity events were often long and dull and inevitably involved wearing uncomfortable "grown-up clothes" and they were a huge part of his life. Likewise, the causes that the Pallisers had long lent a name to often needed signatures, endorsements and other attention that she—if she were his wife—would have to attend to. Such things were almost always at the most inconvenient time and place, but the Pallisers did it because it was their duty. He was used to it because he'd grown up with it.

Emma, on the other hand, would have to change her whole way of living to accommodate other people. She'd never be happy living that way. It would be like keeping a butterfly in a jar...soon all her beautiful colors would fade and her spirit would die.

But if he could get her out of here and take her

back to London they would at least have the chance
to pretend for just a few more days.

She touched his arm. "What's wrong, Brice?" she
asked again, concern coloring her expression.

He looked at her and his heart was full. Unable to
come up with any words, he pulled her into his arms
and kissed her. There was an urgency about it this
time. He had to be with her, had to have her now. It
was almost as if he was afraid she would disappear
if he didn't keep a tight hold on her.

Her kisses were sweet and tender. She was sweet
and tender. She deserved better than Brice.

But he couldn't let her go.

Everything said to him that Emma was the only
thing that would make his life right. But he knew she
wouldn't fit in here. Not because he didn't think she
was able to, but because he didn't think *she* would
want to once she knew what it was like. The closer
she got to the reality of his life, the more she would
hate it. The same way he hated it, at times. He was
selfish to even think of asking her.

There were so many things separating himself and
Emma: cultures, countries, the freedom she was used
to versus the stifled existence of the aristocracy.
Could it ever work between them?

Never, he decided.

He pulled back. "I'm sorry."

"What's to be sorry about?" she asked with a
smile.

He opened the door and they started back out. "A
thousand things," he said and shook his head.

As they stepped out onto the terrace where they

had danced the other night, Emma said, "Your mother isn't crazy about having me here, is she?"

"Don't mind her." They went to the table and he pulled a chair out for Emma to sit. "She's just distracted with organizing this thing. She's had it every year since before I was born. I used to hate this time of year when I was a child because she was impossible to live with."

"You didn't have a very happy childhood, did you?" Emma asked, settling in her seat and watching him as he did the same.

He shook his head. "I'm pretty transparent, aren't I?"

"No, but I always noticed in your letters you avoided the subject. I didn't want to pry—" she stopped and held a palm up "—and I shouldn't pry now, I guess. I just want you to know that I'm always here if you want to talk about it."

She had no idea how much he hoped that was true, but he couldn't bring himself to say so. Instead he said, "Thanks, but there's nothing much to talk about. I mean, you can see what it was." He waved an arm around. "It wasn't *bad*. It wasn't as if I went hungry or cold or anything. Truly, I have no right to complain. It just wasn't particularly *good,* that's all. It was cold, as I told you the other day." *And I've felt the chill ever since.*

Her eyes were warm. It was a stark contrast to the memories that swarmed around him like ghosts. "Whatever it was," she said, "it didn't make *you* cold." She smiled. "There's something to be said for that."

He thought of what John had said to him about how he, Brice, was in a rut, and how the *Independent* had referred to him as heartless. Only Emma saw the man inside.

Only Emma brought the warmth out in him. He *needed* her. He needed to find a way to keep her.

The crazy idea that he could marry her came to him, but he dismissed it just as fast. Even if the marriage was good for him—and he had a hard time believing marriage could be good for anyone—it would be the worst thing he could do to her.

Tea on the terrace consisted of not just tea, but coffee, scones with clotted cream, canapés, fresh fruit, and hot rolls with butter and jam. It was served just as Emma would have pictured high tea, with uniformed staff lifting silver lids off serving dishes and presenting them like precious gems.

As the afternoon light shifted and slanted, tall shadows fell across the pansies and the stone wall. It was bliss.

"We don't normally have a full staff here at Sheldale House, so you should enjoy it while you can," Brice said. "They're here to take care of your every whim."

"I feel funny letting someone else serve me," Emma said, shifting in her seat as a maid refilled her teacup.

"That will be all," Brice said, dismissing the maid.

Emma laughed behind her hand. "You're frighteningly good at that. I never would have guessed you'd have such a commanding air. I don't think I could ever do it."

"Have fun with it," Brice said, brushing it off with a wave of his hand as the maid retreated. "It's what I'm paying them for."

Wholly unfamiliar with the world in which servants attended to one's every need, Emma asked, "What, exactly, do you pay them for?"

He buttered a roll absently. "Hmmm?"

"A huge staff like this in a house with one or two or even ten occupants. What do they do?"

A smile tugged at the corner of his mouth. "Bathe me, dress me, rub my feet and back…"

For a moment, she almost thought he was serious, but his smile gave him away. She raised an eyebrow. "After a long, hard morning of being tangled in the bedsheets?"

His face took on mock concern. "Does that happen to you, too?" He bit into the roll and washed it down with hot tea. "I hate that."

Emma laughed. "Ah, the life of the 'other half.' It's not as easy as everyone thinks, is it?"

"It's true. In all seriousness. You know, there are days when I think if I have to cut through miles of red tape to get the historical society's approval to have one more window fixed in some far-off estate, I'll go mad."

Emma tried to keep a straight face. "Your world is alien to me." There were days when she thought if she had to bag lunch one more time in order to buy a shirt from K mart she, too, would go mad.

His life, whatever the problems and perks, couldn't be more different from hers.

When she'd first walked into the house today, with the earl of Palliser by her side instead of John Turnhill, she'd been overwhelmed by the grandeur. Her instinct had been to turn right around and leave. This kind of opulence wasn't meant for people like her. Every room looked like something out of a decorating book. The kind of fancy coffee-table decorating books that Emma always found too expensive. There was polished woodwork, gilded ceiling frames, tapestries, arching ceilings, tall mirrors and more chintz than she'd ever seen in one place.

She could never live in a place like this, of course. She'd rattle around until she eventually went mad like the first Mrs. Rochester.

"I can't believe you grew up like this," she said, trying to get used to the idea that he didn't live the way she'd thought for so long. "I mean, you've had this your whole life."

"Actually," Brice said seriously. "The staff is a bit of a charade. They've come down from mother's estate in Sheffield. That house, Lansworth, is open to visitors part of every week from April to October."

That surprised her. "*Really?* Like a museum that you pay to get into?"

He shrugged. "A lot of the old house owners do that as a way of trying to keep the expenses under control."

Emma was surprised. "I wouldn't have thought that would be necessary."

"That's the illusion. Most people don't realize it, but every time an estate is passed on, the beneficiary has to pay a death tax of around eighty percent." He shrugged. "And these houses aren't exactly self-sufficient. They're old. Things crumble and break and have to be replaced, often at enormous expense. Yet the house should appear to be the classic English country manor. Visitors and tourists should feel that they are getting a sneaky look at the privileged life, when the truth is that almost no one actually lives that way anymore. You've got to constantly find creative ways to keep up with it."

She thought about it for a moment. "That seems like it could be fun."

He studied her for a moment with a curious expression, then said, "You'd probably be good at it. But not if you had other things to attend to. It can be a lot of work to pile on top of everything else."

Emma looked around. "But why isn't Sheldale House open to the public? I looked into it before I came and it's listed as a private estate, no visitors allowed."

He gave a small shrug. "Believe it or not, Sheldale House is small. The island is small, there wouldn't be enough tourist trade to make it worthwhile. We've got to keep it closed because of insurance issues."

Emma frowned. "Then why doesn't your mother live here instead of in the house that's open to the public?"

He sighed expansively. "Because Lansworth is three times the size—sixty bedrooms, eleven staircases. Even when it's open, it's surprisingly private.''

"So what about your house in London? Do you have people attending to your every need there?''

"I have a staff of four there.'' He smiled. "Even that's more than I really need, but they've been employed by the family for so long that it would be unthinkable for me to let them go.''

At that moment, a maid came out holding a large parcel. She gave it to Brice, who thanked her then she curtsied and went back into the house.

He held the box up, examined the label for a moment, then handed it to Emma. "This is for you,'' he said.

"Me?'' She took the box he put into her hands and looked at the label. "There must be some mistake.''

"There's no mistake.'' His clear, light eyes were crinkled at the corners. "Open it up.''

With one last puzzled look at him, she pulled the wrapping off, and opened the thick corrugated cardboard box. It was full of shredded newspaper. She dug around until her hand touched some fabric, and she pulled out the marionette she had been admiring in the shop Gepetto. "Brice.'' The word came out with a rush of breath. She looked up and saw that he was laughing. "When did you do this?''

"When you went to the bookshop. I had it sent here with the intention of sending it on to you in the States, but,'' he splayed his arms, "here we are.''

"I can't believe this.'' She held the doll up to inspect it in the daylight. "It's even more exquisite than I remembered. Look at this workmanship.'' She handed it to Brice.

He studied it, putting the little mask up to the face and taking it back. "He grows on you. I think I can relate to him."

"I'm beginning to understand why," Emma said soberly. She touched the little porcelain face. "That's probably what appealed to me about him, too. Somewhere inside I knew he was like you." As soon as the words were out of her mouth, she was embarrassed by how silly they sounded. "So," she said, trying to change the subject, "it certainly is a beautiful day." A strong wind picked up, blowing a few stray tendrils of Emma's hair across her face. She brushed them back. "It's going to be tough to get back to work after this."

Brice tapped his fingers against the table. "I wish you weren't leaving," he said quietly. His words lingered in the air for a few beats.

Emma's heart constricted. "I do, too."

He didn't respond, but instead kept looking straight in front of him.

Emma straightened. "But I've got to get back to work. There are several projects waiting for me and, after work hours, I need to start working on those St. Paul's Heart cuttings I'm taking back."

He was thoughtful. "What if you had a job here? Instead of going back to the one in America, I mean."

She laughed. "You don't happen to know someone who's looking for a gardener, do you?"

He turned to her then, and a slow smile came over

his features. "As a matter of fact I do. Are you interested?"

She caught her breath. He wasn't kidding. She suddenly felt she was standing on the edge of a cliff, daring herself to jump. Was this a romantic offer? Or an offer of employment? "That depends on who I'd be working for."

He gave a pirate smile. "A wonderful fellow. Owns one of the properties around here, you may have heard of it."

"Oh?" Her heart pounded so hard she could barely hear above it. In an effort to appear casual, she poured some milk into her Earl Grey tea and stirred slowly, watching the swirl fade.

"Yes. Sheldale House."

"Ah." Emma swallowed. It wasn't merely an offer of employment, he wanted her to stay *with him.* "I've heard of it. I would imagine they were set as far as the gardening staff goes."

Brice leaned forward. "What he's hoping to do is start some kind of laboratory to study the pharmaceutical properties of plants, particularly this St. Paul's Heart. He needs someone to set the whole thing up and staff it."

Her hand, holding a delicate teacup, began to shake. She set the cup down. "Brice, are you serious?"

"I'm deadly serious."

The cliff was real, this truly was a leap to contemplate. "But you don't know anything about the business. You can't do this just for me."

"Why not?" He spoke softly, but with absolute

confidence. "I know enough to believe it's an important and potentially profitable venture. As far as the details go, I defer to you. I trust you completely."

She looked at him and tried to smile, but she was so filled with emotion that all she could say was, "I feel the same way."

He was still for a moment, then gave a slight shake of his head and looked down. "Well," he said, slapping his hands down on top of his thighs. "I've just remembered I forgot to make arrangements for my tux to be cleaned and pressed for tomorrow night. If you'll excuse me, I'd better see to it. Are you comfortable here? Should I have any more tea sent out?"

"No, I'm fine," she said, frowning. What was with the abrupt change of attitude? It was on the tip of her tongue to ask, but she thought better of it. Perhaps it was just her imagination, or she was being oversensitive. After all, the man *did* need his tux tomorrow night. "Don't worry about me," she said.

"We'll finish this conversation later, all right?" he said, raising his eyebrows for her approval. As soon as she gave it with a nod he looked relieved. "Good, then, I'll see you in a little while." With that he was gone, leaving her to wonder if he was afraid *she* was getting too close or, maybe, that *he* was.

After that, the house was abuzz with activity, with everyone getting ready for the party the next night. Emma and Brice barely had another moment alone together, and the ones they did have weren't as relaxed as they should have been. Emma was nervous about going to the party. Really nervous. She'd brushed Brice's concerns away when he'd tried to warn her how out of place she might feel, but now all his words were coming back to her, twice as loud in her mind and twice as ominous as when he'd spoken them.

By early the next night she was practically a wreck. As she changed into her dress, alone in the vast room she'd been sleeping in since she and Brice had moved out of the hotel, she had thoughts of playing sick so she could hide out for the evening. But each thought of hiding was followed by the thought of returning home and regretting forever that she'd given up the opportunity to join Brice at a Cinderella-style ball.

She slipped her nylons on and took her shoes out of her suitcase. They were the last piece of clothing she had to put on before going downstairs. She decided to wait for a moment, and went to sit in the window seat instead.

The sky was deep purple, with a whisper of pink on the horizon. The brick courtyard out front and the long driveway through the trees were lined with lanterns, blazing beautifully along the manicured landscaping. People were arriving in large, gleaming cars that anyone other than Emma might have recognized on sight. Rolls-Royces, she thought, a lot of them were probably Rolls-Royces. She wasn't able to identify them with any certainty, but they were expensive in the way that only old money could afford. There was a lot of old money arriving, she could tell that even from a mile away.

Oddly enough that made her feel more relaxed,

perhaps because of the surreal turn it gave the evening.

There was a knock at the door.

"Yes?" Emma called.

"May I come in?" It was Brice.

"Sure." She got up as the door opened but stopped short when she saw him.

He looked incredible in his tailored black tux, every bit as regal as one would expect an earl to look. She already knew he was handsome—drop-dead gorgeous, in fact—but seeing him in this light made her knees go weak.

"You look beautiful, Emma," he said softly.

"So do you," she breathed.

He laughed and the now-familiar smile was even more handsome than usual. He approached her. "Thanks but I think I'll leave the pretty business to you."

She picked up her shoes and started to put them on, but lost her balance. Brice was quick to put a steadying hand on her shoulder. When she was finished, he held out his elbow to her. "Ready?" he said, cocking his head.

She gave a single nod and tried to breathe past the knot that had formed in her stomach. "Ready."

Emma had no idea how lovely she was, Brice decided as he escorted her into the ballroom. No matter how many times he told her, he knew she would never believe it. Which was fine, really. Her modesty was one of her charms. One of many charms.

As the evening progressed, he saw more of her

charms and talents. Somehow she managed to have an entire conversation with Baron Steinberg, despite the fact that he was as deaf as wood and refused to turn on his hearing aid. She also managed to gracefully avoid the repeated advances of a distant relative of the family, a man who was known for crashing society parties and overindulging in drink, without once offending him, though Brice thought the man richly deserved offense.

Somehow she even managed to engage the elderly dowager, Madame Boulrais, in a conversation about the merits of homeopathy which ended with the old woman asking Emma for her telephone number in the States so she could call with further questions about treating her bursitis. Brice couldn't recall ever seeing the dowager smile before, much less ask for a telephone number. In fact, he was somewhat surprised that she even owned a telephone.

In short, Emma was, literally, the belle of the ball. In a situation that he would have bet money she'd hate, she'd thrived. He'd underestimated her. But of course, he reminded himself, this was only one night. Emma might enjoy herself less if she were doing this sort of thing on a regular basis. In fact, he was sure she would come to detest it—so he'd better make the most of tonight.

When the orchestra began playing *Isn't it Romantic,* Brice interrupted Emma's conversation with the earl of Menthorpe and asked her to dance.

She accepted gladly. ''I told him over and over again that herbal therapy for back pain was *not* the same as massage and that I wasn't able to speak with authority on either, but he was determined." She laughed. "In truth, I don't think his back is his problem at all."

Brice laughed and pulled her closer, loving the feel of her warmth against him. "So you see what I mean about dealing with these people, then. It can be a nightmare."

She shrugged. "It's kind of fun, though. Where else do you run into such characters outside of a Jane Austen novel? That reminds me, I was talking to someone about a books-for-kids program you're sponsoring."

He thought for a moment. "That would be Agatha Rainstrem. The Literature Society."

"Right. Very nice woman."

She'd always struck Brice as something of a shrew, but he nodded.

"Anyway, I had an idea. Sort of a brainstorm." Emma's face was alight with enthusiasm. "What if you had a writing contest for kids? You know, best essay wins publication in the local newspaper and library supplies for his or her school. What do you think?"

He stopped and took a step back from Emma to look at her. "You're not going to believe this, but I had almost the exact same idea. Agatha wouldn't even listen to it."

Emma frowned. "That's strange. She seemed really interested when I mentioned it just now."

"You're kidding."

"No, I mean it. She said she was going to take the idea to the next meeting."

Brice pulled her close again and they danced some more. "You're amazing, Emma. Truly." An uncomfortable twinge twisted in his chest. "Let's go get some champagne."

Emma couldn't believe how much fun she was having. She couldn't remember ever enjoying herself this much at a party, much less at a formal party as large as this. It had to be because of the fact that Brice was by her side, she concluded as he handed her a crystal flute of champagne.

"To you," he said, clinking his glass against hers.

"And you," she added, then sipped. It was dry and toasty and marvelous, tickling down her throat in a mouthful of tiny bubbles.

"Brice!" a female voice suddenly said.

Emma started.

Brice froze.

They both turned to face a tall blond woman in a red dress, undoubtedly made by a designer, probably for her personally. She was smiling, a dazzling straight white smile. "For the love of God, Brice, where have you been? Do you have any idea what I've been going through trying to find you these past couple of weeks?"

Brice looked like he was viewing a ghost. "Ah...I've been busy."

"I should think so! I've been asking everyone, and I must say tongues were wagging behind me. A girl can look pretty foolish just by virtue of being associated with you."

Lillian Palliser appeared behind the woman.

"Look who's here, Brice, it's Caroline. I wasn't sure she was going to make it, but here she is."

"I'm on my way to France," she said, looking steadily at Brice. "I have a *very important date* there."

Emma heard his teeth click together. He said to the woman, Caroline, "Good. We need to talk. *Now.*" He looked at Emma. "Will you excuse me for just a moment?"

Emma moved her champagne flute from one hand to the other. "Of course."

The woman looked at Emma as well then. "Gosh, I'm sorry, I didn't realize—"

Whatever else she was going to say was lost as Brice pulled her by the arm. "We've got to do this *fast*," he said to her. "Emma, stay put, I'll be right back."

"Brice, what's the matter with you?" the woman asked. "Aren't you even going to introduce me to your friend? Honestly, what's gotten into you?"

"Never mind that now." He guided her away from the group. "What are you doing here?" Emma heard him ask.

"Billy and I are going to France so we can..." They disappeared through the door to the hall.

Emma stood, bemused. Who was Caroline? Why hadn't Brice introduced them? More to the point, why had he ushered her off in that secretive way? She didn't seem troubled by the fact that Emma was there, so she probably wasn't a scorned lover or anything, but still, it was very odd that he hadn't introduced them.

Do you have any idea what I've been going through trying to find you? Why was she trying to find him? Emma took a deep breath. Brice would be out in a minute or two and he'd clear it up then.

She waited, her trepidation growing with every passing minute. Brice's mother was making small talk at her side. "Now where on earth have Brice and Caroline gone?"

Emma's heart began to pound. Something was really wrong. "I'm sure they'll be right back," she answered, surprised at how weak her own voice sounded.

Lillian clucked her tongue and took a step closer to Emma, the scent of her perfume drifting headily between them. There was a note of jasmine, Emma noticed, trying to cling to any small comfortable thought.

"Honestly, that boy," Lillian went on. "He's behaving so oddly lately." She seemed to be talking more to herself than to Emma. "Ah, well, Caroline will get him straightened out. She always does."

A sick feeling grew in Emma's stomach. The jasmine scent suddenly seemed rancid. "I'm afraid I'm not exactly sure who Caroline is," she ventured carefully, trying her hardest to keep her voice steady.

Lillian looked genuinely surprised, then clucked her tongue again. "Caroline Fortescue," she said, indicating the direction Brice and Caroline had gone. "I'll introduce you properly when they return." She shook her head. "This is exactly the kind of thing I've noticed about him lately. He's barely seen to the poor girl, and he never even mentions the marriage."

Emma swallowed, then swallowed again. "Marriage?" she repeated at last.

Lillian nodded. "Brice and Caroline's."

That fell like a brick into Emma's stomach. She could barely find her voice. "I'm sorry, I don't mean to appear dense, but...Brice and Caroline are getting married?"

"Of course," the older woman said. "Oh, dear, didn't you realize? Caroline Fortescue is Brice's fiancée."

Chapter Nine

Brice's mind raced as he and Caroline walked into the drawing room. He glanced behind him once as they left the ballroom and thought Emma looked a little disconcerted, though he wasn't sure if it was from his departure or the fact that she was standing next to his mother.

He wished he could just take Emma and sweep her back to London, away from his real life and obligations, away from his mother and her expectations, away from everything that had constituted his life for the past thirty-six years. But he'd have to go farther than London for that. He'd have to go to the moon.

He hadn't thought much of it before, but lately he was coming to realize that his life was not a terribly happy one. Before Emma had come along, he had gone about his business as he always had, never stopping to question his own emotions, or the lack of them.

What would happen when Emma was gone again? What would his life be? He recalled Socrates' cave: those within, who had never seen the light, lived contentedly in their sheltered environment. But those who caught even a glimpse of the light never wanted to go back.

The cave wasn't enough anymore.

Emma was the light. How was he going to live without it, now that he had seen it?

He shook his head. Why was he getting sentimental now? They couldn't have a future together, that was certain. After all, it wasn't as if anything in his life could change to accommodate a free spirit like her. She'd be miserable if she stayed with him. She'd probably want to run away and never look back.

"Okay, Brice, what's going on?" Caroline asked, looking at the Rolex watch on her wrist.

He moved away and sat on the edge of the desk. "We've got to come clean about our supposed engagement."

"You're telling me." She rolled her eyes. "As a matter-of-fact, I wanted to talk to you about that very thing."

"You did?"

She nodded. "Billy and I are going to France to be married."

Brice sighed with relief. "So you didn't need me for cover anymore anyway."

"Nope. Truthfully, I was worried that you were going to be miffed at me for dropping this on you."

"What, because you're dumping me for your pool boy?"

She laughed. "He was my riding instructor, and *yes.*"

"Well, he's a better man than I am," Brice replied gallantly. "I wish you the best, Caro, I really do."

"Thanks, darling." She smiled, her blue eyes wide. "So when do we tell them the truth? Tonight?"

He nodded. "Now."

"How?"

He stood from where he'd been sitting on the corner of his desk. "I don't have a brilliant plan for breaking it to everyone," he said. He began to pace. "But I'm willing to take the blame for the dissolution."

She eyed him. "You do realize that that means a transfer of funds? Our fathers drew up that contract for us years ago." She shook her head. "It's so medieval, isn't it?"

"Yes," he agreed. He'd known about the contract from his early years. Drawn up in a drunken stupor, the paper had represented their fathers' hopes for doubling their fortunes. If either party was to back out, it would mean they owed the other half a million pounds. "I don't care what the price is," Brice said, meaning it. "I'll pay it."

Caroline whistled. "You know, if there was anything I could do about that I would," she said. "But with Daddy's lawyer still alive and kicking, I don't think you're going to get away with anything."

"I don't care," he said.

Caroline stood up and went to Brice. "I know why *I* want to stop this, but why do *you?* Does it by any chance have anything to do with the girl in there?'' she asked, gesturing toward the ballroom. ''The one you should have introduced me to, but didn't?''

''Some, yes,'' he confessed. ''But it's also that I've got to live honestly from now on. I can't keep up with the lie.''

She laughed. ''It never suited you, darling.'' She laid a hand on his shoulder. ''Are you going to marry her?''

''I can't.''

She moved her hand to her hip and frowned. ''Why ever not?''

''She'd be miserable.''

Caroline quirked her lips. ''Did you ask, or have you decided that for her?''

He started to answer, then stopped. His stomach tightened. ''Look,'' he said to Caroline. ''I just need to go in there and get this over with.''

''Suits me fine. Do you want me to come with you to help explain?'' she asked kindly.

He gave her a brief smile. She'd always been a good friend to him. ''No, thanks. You have an important date, don't you? You can probably slip out the kitchen door without running into anyone. I can take care of our 'engagement' myself. And I'll have Olivia plant something in the papers about how I've wronged you.''

''Okay.'' She shrugged, then went over and gave him a kiss on the cheek. ''Thanks, darling.''

He started toward the door, but she stopped him. ''Brice.''

He turned around, a little impatiently. ''Yes?''

"If you love her, and she loves you, then trust her. Don't make decisions for her."

By the time he reached his mother and Emma, his ears were burning. The look on Emma's face said it all.

"Where did Caroline go?" his mother asked, oblivious to the emotionally charged air around them.

He looked at Lillian. "She had a date." He looked back at Emma. Her eyes were bright and her face pale. "Mother, could you excuse Emma and me?"

"Certainly," she said, waving a hand to indicate that they should step away rather than her.

He didn't have time to feel irritated with her. Instead he went to Emma and took her by the arm to guide her out to the terrace. "Please?" he said softly. "I need to talk to you."

She stood with a sigh and walked with him, but she didn't meet his eyes. "Your mother was just telling me about Caroline," she said, but her voice faltered. "That she's your fiancée."

"She's not." She glanced at him and he continued. "That's the short answer. That's the part I want you to hear first."

She looked straight ahead again. "So, what's the long answer?"

"The long answer is that it was never a real engagement." The evening air was crisp when they stopped out. "Caroline and I have known each other since we were children, but we never had any intention of going through with the marriage. Our parents decreed it years ago and it's just been easier for both of us not to argue.''

''To lie.''

He held up a finger. ''To let them believe what they wanted to believe until it came time to face the battle that the truth will undoubtedly instigate.''

She looked at him incredulously. ''Brice, for a guy who supposedly values the truth so much, you certainly are economical with it.''

''I realize it seems that way, but...'' He shrugged. ''I don't know why you would believe me, but I'm telling the truth. You happen to have witnessed the only real deceptions I've ever committed. My life is...it's very complicated.''

She shifted her weight and eyed him. ''That's quite a coincidence,'' she said skeptically.

He ignored that. ''Caroline and I have agreed to tell the truth. In fact, I would have told my mother just now, but I thought it was more important to talk to you about it first.''

She hesitated. ''Should I believe that?''

He sensed her relenting. ''You can come with me right now and watch me tell her.''

She took a trembling breath. ''And what will you tell her about me?''

''That,'' he touched her chin, ''is up to you. Are you staying?''

Her eyes softened then, and the expression reached right into his chest and grabbed him by the heart. ''What, exactly, are you asking me?''

He froze. She thought he was proposing marriage.

* * *

He hesitated and Emma knew in that moment that he hadn't been proposing, but that they both knew she thought he was. She was instantly embarrassed by her question. "Never mind, I didn't ask."

"There's nothing I'd like more than to be able to…to give that to you," Brice said. "But I can't."

She looked down. She didn't want to look petulant, but she was too humiliated to meet his eyes. "No, that's okay. I know you never said you loved me." *That's one lie I can't hold you responsible for, I told it to myself.*

"I do…care…a great deal about you."

Her heart stung. The words had a hollow ring to them. "But…?"

"The problem is that you know me as someone with a simple life with the same freedom you have, and that's not who I am. Our life together couldn't be what you want it to be, not if we were married."

"So what were you offering when you asked me to stay?"

"Exactly what I said. To set up a lab here, to have you run it."

"That's it? All business?" She sniffed and tried to hold her tears back. "Because I didn't get that from you, that your only interest in me was business."

"It's not," he said softly. "I wanted to keep you here to be with me, too. I'd be lying if I didn't admit that."

She gave a bitter laugh. "You wouldn't want to *lie* now, would you?"

He wiped a tear off her cheek and kissed the place that it had been. "Emma, that's not fair."

She looked at him hotly. "What you're saying is that you want to keep me here but not make any sort of commitment. That would make me sort of like a— a prostitute."

"Emma—"

"Is that what you think of me?"

"Of course not, don't put words in my mouth." His voice hardened.

"What would you call it?"

"I didn't think that living with me constituted prostitution."

"No, normally it constitutes being a wife," she said. She didn't understand the distinction he was making. "So what you're saying is that we *can't* get married because that would make things too complicated, but we can live together and everything will be hunky dory?"

His shoulders sagged fractionally. "If you married me, you'd become a Palliser and, in that very moment, you would have more tedious obligations and duties than you can even imagine. This is the worst part of my deception, Emma. I wasn't able to make you understand that whole part of my life, and now I'm trying to explain it in a nutshell and it sounds trite."

"So what you're saying is that you're protecting me."

"I guess you could put it that way."

This turn of events was difficult to grasp. "You

want to marry me, but you don't want to put *me* through that."

"Exactly." His voice was sincere. He looked pained. "I know this is difficult. Believe me, it's difficult for me, too."

"Then let me decide for myself."

"I can't do that to you."

Tears stung at her eyes. "Why not?"

"Because I know you would be miserable." His voice held no emotion.

"How could you know that?"

He moved over to her and put an arm around her, pulling her toward him. "Emma," he whispered. "You've got to trust that I know this life. And you don't. I know what it would entail, and I know you well enough to know that it wouldn't make you happy."

"So you won't even give me a chance to prove you wrong?" she asked, realizing in the back of her mind, even as she said it, that she couldn't change his mind. He was honorable enough that he wouldn't do anything he thought would damage her, and he seemed genuinely to believe that becoming his wife would damage her.

There was a long silence.

"I'm sorry," he said again. "Because I do love you."

"Don't say that," she said, crossing her arms in front of her as if that would keep her emotions in check.

"It's true."

She wiped the tears off her cheeks angrily. She started to leave. "I'm going."

"Going where?"

"Back to London. Back home. I don't think I can take any more of this." She sniffed. "Please give your mother my regrets."

She started again to go, but he was behind her in an instant, turning her around. "Emma, please don't go."

"I can't stay." But she stilled in his arms.

He gave her a penetrating gaze. "You have my heart, you have my very soul. I would gladly give it all to you. There's just one thing that I can't give you."

"Marriage," she said, with a resigned nod.

"Doesn't love mean anything to you?"

She looked at him for a long time. Finally she said, "Not your kind of love. Maybe you thought I was different. More modern or more independent or something, but I'm an old-fashioned girl. I want the whole fairy tale or nothing." She looked at him without bitterness. "I'm sorry."

She turned and hurried away, leaving him standing there, staring after her. She'd come so close to being Cinderella, but it had stopped short. She was running away from the ball in her beautiful gown, but Prince Charming had already told her that he didn't want her.

Three and a half hours later she was on the late ferry back to the mainland. Brice hadn't tried to stop her again and it was just as well. She knew that he wasn't going to say what she needed to hear.

He'd offered to drive her to the port himself, but she'd refused. He'd offered his driver, and she'd refused that, too. Finally, he had given up and let her take a taxi.

The sadness in his eyes the last time she had looked at him was almost enough to break her heart, had it not already been broken. She believed his intentions were good. She believed he really thought he was saving her from a fate worse than...well, worse than whatever fate awaited her when she went back home. Probably an endless string of Friday movie nights with the girls, eating food that wasn't healthy for them and lamenting the fact that there were no good men out there.

She didn't look forward to it.

Emma settled down in her seat, glancing around to see if anyone was close enough to notice her. There was an older couple at the far end of the cabin. The man was asleep and the woman was reading a tabloid newspaper.

There was no one else around, thank goodness. At least she had some privacy for her misery. She looked out at the calm water beyond. What was left for her now?

The days of finding a letter from England waiting for her at the end of a long day's work were over. John Turnhill no longer existed. A knot found its way into Emma's throat. Where John had been there would now be a big hole in her life. She took a shaking breath. Live and learn, she tried to tell herself. But the sense of loss was overwhelming.

She kept her focus on the sea. Soon it all began to blur, and hot tears filled her eyes and ran, unchecked, down her cheeks.

Brice tried to tell himself that he'd expected Emma's leaving. Ever since he'd met her in London he'd known, somewhere inside, that he was going to have to tell her the truth about who he was eventually, and that the truth would end it all. He'd *known* it, so he could accept it, right? He just had to concentrate on other things, like his work.

The end of the ball had been as catastrophic as the beginning had been pleasant. He'd told his mother about himself and Caroline, and she hadn't taken it well, though she didn't lash out about Emma with the venom that he had imagined. Instead she'd decided to blame Caroline for marrying her riding instructor. Perhaps it was easier for her to believe her son had been jilted, practically at the altar, than to believe he'd never wanted to marry the Fortescue fortune in the first place.

But far worse than enduring that conversation with his mother was enduring the knowledge that Emma was upstairs packing her things and calling a taxi so she could leave, and that she wouldn't talk to him, no matter what he had to say.

All in all, the night had been agony.

When he got back to his London house the next morning, he called the office and got an update on everything that had happened during his absence. His secretary didn't have anything terribly important to relate, but he told her he was coming back Tuesday morning anyway.

"So early, sir?"

"It's not that early," he said curtly.

His secretary, Olivia, had known him for a long time. "You weren't planning on coming back until the middle of the week." Her tone turned motherly. "And I must say, you don't sound very rested from your vacation. Why don't you enjoy the rest of your time off? It's the first holiday you've taken in at least the three years I've been here."

And probably the last. "I'll be in at 8:00 a.m. Schedule an appointment with Beckworth. We need to review those projected numbers. Oh, and put something in the papers about me cheating on Caroline…or something." He hung the phone up before she could give further protest.

It would be a relief to be back at work. It felt good just to be back in London, where he could follow some semblance of his routine. He breathed deeply.

Emma was still in London.

Not that it mattered. He was just in shock because of the scene they'd gone through. By Tuesday morning he would be feeling much more himself. By then she'd have left, and the heart-wrenching idea of her being within several miles of him would no longer be a problem.

He shifted uneasily. As soon as he'd had some time to cool down, this urge to follow her and track her down wouldn't exist any longer. Life would be back to normal.

Four hours later he realized that, in his efforts to stop thinking about her, he had thought of nothing but her. She wasn't just any woman and she never had been. He'd known it from the beginning. There was no way on earth he could do without her. It had been foolish to even think that.

Over the past two years, he realized now, he had fallen in love with her. During this week he had come to understand that it was real. Nothing else he had ever experienced came close to it, and no woman he had ever met was anything like Emma.

She was one of a kind. And she was gone—because he hadn't trusted her to make her own decision about what she wanted to do with her life. She was a strong woman, fully capable of taking care of herself. She didn't need him to protect her. Good Lord, it was one of the things he loved about her.

Maybe it was his own fear that had allowed him to let her go. Hadn't the ball proved his fears groundless? After all, Emma had been a huge success and hadn't seemed the least bit bored with even the stodgiest of guests. Maybe she *could* handle this life of his. Or maybe she could change it. One thing he knew was that life with Emma would be fun. It would be fulfilling. It would be the opposite of what it had been for thirty-six years.

She'd turned his world upside down and shaken the change out of its pockets. He liked that. Things that used to matter a great deal to him suddenly didn't seem so important when he compared them with Emma. Even if he gave up a few responsibilities to make life more fun it wouldn't mean his demise. He would be rich in love.

He had to tell her.

He took out the London phone directory and looked up the hotel where Emma had been staying. Heart pounding, he dialed the number.

A woman answered after the first ring. "Sunnington Hotel."

"Good evening. I wonder if you can tell me if a Ms. Emma Lawrence has booked a room there for this evening."

There was a hesitation on the other end of the line. "Who's calling?"

"Brice Palliser," he answered, without thinking.

"Oh! Lord Palliser? My husband works for your company!" The bubbly woman's voice turned skeptical. "Is this really Lord Palliser?"

"Yes." He was irritated. "Could you just tell me if Ms. Lawrence is there this evening?"

"As a matter of fact, she checked in last night. Would you like me to go to her room and fetch her?"

Brice sucked a breath in through his teeth. It would be a mistake to warn her that he was coming. If she knew that he knew where to find her, she'd probably register in one of London's millions of other hotels. "Don't get her," he said quickly. "In fact, I'd really prefer that you don't tell her I called. This is…a surprise."

The woman lowered her voice. "I won't breathe a word."

He hoped she wouldn't.

Chapter Ten

That morning, Emma decided to check out of the Sunnington. She'd managed to change her airline reservation by a day with no penalty, and she was glad to take it. London had lost its glow for her, literally and figuratively. It had been raining ever since she'd arrived the previous evening, and the newspaper weather report predicted more of the same for the entire workweek. It definitely seemed like an omen.

She packed her bags and went down to the lobby. The young man who had been there when Emma had checked in was gone. The kind proprietress in his place looked almost stricken when Emma said she was leaving early.

"You're leaving now?"

"I am, yes."

"I hope it's not a problem with the accommodations," she said, with a question in her voice and a surreptitious glance around the lobby.

"Not at all," Emma said quickly. "The room was perfect. I hope to come back here sometime soon." It was a small lie, but a white one.

The woman's face took on a mousy anxiety, and she continued to glance right and left. Emma figured she was worried other guests or a potential guest would hear and suspect there was something wrong with the hotel. "If the rate is the problem, I'd be glad to work some new figures out for you."

Emma smiled. "That's very sweet, but honestly there's no problem." She raised her voice slightly, to reassure the woman that anyone overhearing their conversation would think nothing was wrong with the accommodations. "I'm meeting someone," she said. "He's taking me to the airport to go home today."

The woman relaxed. "Ah, meeting someone, are you?" She raised an eyebrow. "A certain gentleman, by any chance?"

Emma hesitated. The woman was probably concerned about her traveling alone. What the heck? If it would give her peace of mind she'd tell her she was meeting Hercules. "Yes, I'm meeting him right down the street," she assured her, hoping she wouldn't ask for further details. "In fact, I'd better hurry if I want to get there on time."

"Very good." The proprietress gave an exaggerated wink. "You have a wonderful time." Then she added, "You know, lots of girls would envy you your luck."

Emma frowned, but decided not to ask what the woman meant and run the risk of finding herself engaged in a filibuster. The sooner she could get away from London and all its memories, the sooner she would start to feel better.

Brice went to the garage and took out his car. It was eleven o'clock in the morning. The clock on his desk had been slow, and he'd thought he had much more time to make it to Emma's hotel while she was still eating breakfast. Now, if he drove like a demon, he might just get to the hotel before she went out for the day.

He thought about what he'd say when he saw her. It would have to be good. He'd never proposed to a woman before, and this instance was particularly tricky since he'd effectively *un*proposed to her the day before. He'd have to make this perfect. A two-knee beg. He only hoped she'd forgive him for everything he'd done wrong up to this point.

The heirloom Palliser engagement ring that had been in his family for six generations felt heavy in his pocket as he barreled uncertainly into his future, but he knew it would feel heavier still if Emma turned him down.

The train sped through the dark cavern of the underground system. Emma settled in one of the uncomfortable seats and looked at her watch. 11:05 a.m. Her plane didn't leave until 3:25. She couldn't wait to get on it and leave the shores of England far behind at five hundred miles per hour. Unfortunately, even that wasn't fast enough to leave her memories behind.

She didn't want to go to the airport this early, she thought. Airports were full of lovers. Lovers running into each other's arms after time apart, lovers weeping copiously as they had to say goodbye. She just didn't think she could stand that today.

It would do her considerably more good to stop somewhere for coffee and say goodbye to London in her own private way. Even so, she tried to talk herself out of her next move.

She couldn't. Unable to resist the draw of the restaurant Brice had taken her to on their first night together, she stood up, took her suitcase and moved toward the door, waiting for the stop.

This is crazy, she told herself. Then again, maybe it wasn't. Maybe going there again would act as a kind of exorcism for her, to get Brice and the memory of him out of her system once and for all. It seemed unlikely, she had to admit, but her instincts were drawing her there so she decided to follow them and see what kind of emotional ride they took her on.

Something told her if she didn't go this morning, she would always wish she had.

The train bumped along, and Emma watched the dark walls whiz past. She felt numb. The clatter of the rails beneath the train spoke to her, taunting, "You're running away, you're running away." Maybe she was, but she didn't see what alternative she had. If she'd stayed on, living with Brice in an uncommitted, undefinable relationship, she would have given up her own integrity. She could survive without Brice, though the loss was going to be difficult, especially at first. Somehow, someday, she'd come to terms with it. She *couldn't* survive without her self-respect.

Brice stopped a street vendor near the hotel and bought a bouquet of carnations for Emma. He took a deep breath for courage, and stepped into the Sunnington.

He went to the desk. "I'm Brice Palliser," he began. "I'm here to—"

The woman behind the desk was immediately flustered. "Sir! My goodness, what an honor it is to have you here."

He smiled, a bit nervously. Emma was just a few steps away now. "I spoke with someone earlier. I'm here to see Emma Lawrence. Could you tell me which room she's in?"

The woman's face fell. "Emma Lawrence?"

"That's right."

"But she's gone. She left this morning. I thought she was meeting *you.*"

He felt like he'd been punched in the stomach. "Gone? Where did she go?"

"Why, to the airport." The woman colored. "She said she had to meet someone who was driving her there. After your call, I assumed she meant you."

"The airport!"

She nodded.

"Bloody hell," he muttered, for once heedless of propriety. That couldn't be right. Her flight wasn't due to leave from London until the next afternoon. "Are you sure?"

"Absolutely."

"Did she say what time her flight was?"

The woman shook her head. "No. All she said was that she was going home."

"Damn it!" He looked up at the woman's surprise. "Excuse me. Thank you for your help." He strode out of the lobby and threw the flowers on the pavement. Why the hell had Emma changed her flight? Couldn't she stick around just one more day?

She was probably flying with the same airline, he thought, and tried to remember which it had been. Daily flights tended to leave at the same time. He picked up his car phone and called the operator to get the number, then dialed it.

The flight was leaving at 3:25. He looked at the clock on the dash. It was 11:25 now. He had some time. His breath left in a long stream. She'd be at the airport, of course. Where else would she go? She'd check in and then wait by the gate for announcements.

It wouldn't take him more than forty-five minutes to get to the airport in the traffic that was out today. Maybe even less. He could make it. He had to make it.

After all this, he wasn't about to lose her now.

She thought she'd be okay. She'd honestly thought seeing the place again would make her feel better. It didn't. As she approached the restaurant, her chest began to ache and her eyes burned. The sky was clearing up and people sat at the outdoor tables, plates and utensils dinged through the quiet hush of talking and cars passing. It was a cheerful sound, but this morning it only made Emma feel like an outsider.

A lump in her throat grew and threatened to choke her. Finally she had to give in to it. She sat on a bench on the street and let the tears come.

When she had cried herself dry, Emma went on over to the café, where she would have some coffee and a croissant and begin the rest of her life right. No matter what, she was determined that she wasn't going to indulge in thoughts of Brice Palliser anymore. It was an episode in her life that someday, with time and distance, would probably bring a smile to her face. At any rate, it would amuse her grandchildren if she ever had any.

Grandma once had a pen pal who was an earl and she didn't know it. When they met, he pretended to be someone else until his cover was blown. He showed her his ancestral estates. She saw Remington paintings, and Renoir paintings, and even a Vincent Van Gogh up close. The earl and Grandma drank Dom Perignon champagne together.

Oh, and the earl said he loved Grandma.

Once upon a time, a long, long time ago.

Parking at the airport was a nightmare. It took almost half an hour to park, when it should have taken no more than ten minutes. Fortunately, the space wasn't too far from the terminal. Brice shoved his keys in his pocket and ran for it.

He went straight to the airline check-in, certain

that she would be right there. When she wasn't, he floundered. He didn't have a back-up plan.

He looked at every face in the waiting area, then in the surrounding area, then at the baggage checks and the skycap stations. He tried everything, including the shops and food courts. She was nowhere.

He went back to the airline clerk and asked, "Has Emma Lawrence checked in yet?"

"I'm sorry, sir, but we're not permitted to give out that information."

"Please," he said, trying the smile Caroline had always told him would charm the birds out of the trees if only he'd use it once in a while. "I've got to catch this woman before she goes back to America or else two lives are going to be ruined."

The girl raised a skeptical brow. "You're going to have to do better than that." Then she waited.

He raked his hand across his hair wearily. "The truth is I want to propose to her, but when I went to her hotel she was already gone and this is the only other place I could think to look."

She clearly wanted to believe him. "Is that the truth?"

All his vehemence had left him. "Yes," he said simply.

She assessed him for a long moment, and he was about to turn and walk away when she said, "What's the name?"

He turned back. "Emma Lawrence."

She scanned the list on the computer screen before her. "What was the last name again?"

"Lawrence?"

"Could she be traveling under any other name, like a married name? Maiden name?"

"No, that's her name." He tried to peer at the computer screen himself. "Could you look again?"

He looked at his watch as she checked the list again. It was twelve-thirty. The plane was leaving in three hours. If she were here she wouldn't be sitting around without checking in first.

With a shrug the clerk turned back to Brice with the same blank look. "I'm sorry there's no one by that name on the reservations list."

Utterly deflated, he turned and walked away.

Where could he look for her now? The woman at the hotel had been certain Emma had gone to the airport, but now the woman from the airline was equally certain she wasn't here. One thing was certain, she wasn't in either place.

Disheartened, he wandered back to his car and got in. He had no idea where to go now, or what to do with himself. He'd been such a fool, this was probably exactly what he deserved. Then again, maybe it was all just bad luck.

He began driving and found himself, forty minutes later, pulling into the block in Hampstead Heath where *La Fontaine du Mars* was, the place where he'd first been with Emma. Maybe he was a glutton for punishment, but somehow coming here made him feel closer to her.

He parked the car near where he'd parked with Emma that night and retraced their steps to the restaurant. It had been a gloomy day, but the sun was poking out from behind the steely clouds and the

outdoor tables were set up and there were people
sitting outside, chatting and laughing as though the
world hadn't just become a dismal place.

Barely paying attention to his surroundings, he
plodded to the tables, sat at the first one he came to,
and asked the waitress for a cup of coffee.

The waitress offered to refill Emma's cup and she
nodded. She'd already had a lot of caffeine, and
probably shouldn't have any more, but at least it was
something to do. She had more than a couple of
hours before her flight left, and she couldn't just sit
at the café table without ordering anything.

She didn't know what had made her come back to
the little bistro after the torrent of tears she'd shed
across the street. Something had just told her it was
best. Rather than turning away from her thoughts, she
had to face them head-on. This was as good a place
as any. Perhaps better, because they'd been here together before he'd told her the truth about his identity. Before it became obvious they had no future
together.

She'd been here for half an hour already, though,
and so far she didn't feel exorcized. In fact, she was
thinking of him more than ever, and it was getting
more and more difficult to maintain her anger. The
sun had come out, and it seemed even crueler than
the rain. She didn't want to leave. Part of her *never*
wanted to leave this beautiful country.

She picked at the flaky, buttery croissant on the
table before her. Brice's proposition that she stay and
live with him was unacceptable, that wouldn't

change. She would never be able to live happily under those conditions. But he hadn't intended it as an insult. He'd seen it as a viable way for them to spend time together. Whatever his reasons for thinking a marriage would make her miserable, they had to be pretty compelling to him because he had truly looked tortured when Emma had left.

She took a sip of hot black coffee and it burned down her throat. Had she really done the right thing? Uncertainty wavered in her. Maybe it wouldn't be so bad to just live with him, at least that way she'd have some time with him. She drank again, then set the cup down with a definitive thunk. No, she couldn't stay. It would be damaging to herself and, ultimately, their relationship. Better to leave it as a fond memory.

"Excuse me," a voice called behind her, cutting through the soft din of murmured conversation. Emma straightened. It was a familiar voice. "Coffee, please." The waitress nodded to the person and Emma heard. "Thank you."

She froze. Her heart pounded, but she couldn't get herself to turn around. Brice wouldn't be here. He was in Guernsey, fulfilling his obligations. What could he possibly be doing in Hampstead Heath?

A cup was set down. "Here you are, sir. Is there anything else?"

She was able to pick out his response through the noise. "No, that will be all."

This time she was sure.

Emma turned around. Several tables of people separated them, but suddenly a woman laughed and leaned slightly to the side. And there he was, Brice Palliser, not more than twelve feet away. Their eyes locked. Her heart thundered in her chest. *Get out,* a voice inside shouted. *Get out of here while you still can. Don't talk to him. Don't look at him.* But she couldn't move. It was an incredibly awkward moment. How could fate have humiliated her by bringing him here, now, when all she wanted to do was get quietly out of the country?

"Emma." His lips formed the word, but no sound came out. He got up and moved toward her.

Her breath became shallow. "What are you doing here?" she managed.

Without taking his eyes off her, he stopped before her, and laid a hand to her cheek. "Is it really you?"

"What are you doing here?" she repeated, louder now. His touch was warm, and all too comforting.

"I was looking for you." His eyes were wide with disbelief. "After the woman at your hotel told me you'd gone to the airport, I spent the morning stopping strange women with auburn hair in the terminal."

"Why?" She tried to make her tone chilly, but she couldn't.

"Isn't it obvious?" He took both of her hands in his. "I need you, Emma. If you go, it's going to tear a hole in my heart." He pulled her out of her chair and into a strong embrace. "I love you."

"I love you, too, Brice. But that doesn't make everything all right."

"Everything is different now," he said, running his hand up and down her back.

"It is?"

He pulled away and nodded, looking deep into her eyes. "I want you to stay. Forever."

"I've already told you I can't compromise."

"I won't ask you to. I don't *want* you to."

She swallowed. "Won't that complicate things?"

"Undoubtedly."

"And you don't mind?"

"Not if you don't. It will be a dramatic change from the life you're used to. What do you say?"

She narrowed her eyes at him. There was no way she was going to make the same stupid mistake twice. "What, exactly, are you asking?"

He smiled and got on one knee before her. He took her hand and pressed it to his lips then slid the heirloom ring on her finger with a questioning gaze. "I'm asking you, Emma Lawrence, if you will do me the honor of becoming my wife. I know I'm not worthy—"

"Yes!" The word was out before she even realized what she was saying. Conversation stilled around them. He stood and she threw her arms around his neck. "Yes," she said again.

He kissed her, passionately. She could hear the whispered voices around them, but she didn't care. Everything was falling into place. Every part of her that had ached and felt hollow just ten minutes ago was soothed and filled with the warmest feeling of bliss.

At last he pulled back and looked into her eyes. "Are you sure about this? Because once we're married we're staying that way."

Her face was glowing, she could feel it. "I'm positive. Are you?"

He kissed her gently on each cheek. "I've never been more certain of anything. I want to marry you, Emma. I want to live with you forever. I want to have ten children together."

She raised a brow, still smiling. "Ten?"

He shrugged. "Well, we'll start with one at a time."

"Ah, the old-fashioned way."

He smiled. "The point is, without you in my life I have nothing." He bent down and put his mouth over hers. The kiss was deliriously long and dizzying. When he pulled away and looked into her eyes, his own were bright. Then he turned to the waitress, who was standing by, watching, her own eyes bright with sentiment. "Mimosas all around," he said in a loud voice, with a sweep of his arm. "This is a celebration."

The waitress hurried inside, as the patrons made sounds of pleasure and wonder at Brice's offer.

"What's the occasion?" a voice called cheerfully.

Brice pulled Emma close. "We're getting married."

A whoop of cheers went up around them and the wait staff came out with bottles of champagne and orange juice. When everyone who wanted a drink had one, a stout man with a handlebar mustache set down his copy of the *Independent* and stood up, holding his glass high. "To the bride and groom, then."

People raised their glasses.

Brice turned to Emma and gently clinked his glass against hers and smiled. ''Dear Emma,'' he said softly in her ear, so no one except her could hear him. ''The most amazing change has come over me since I last wrote to you...''

Epilogue

Emma stood at the back of the five-hundred-year-old church in Guernsey and peered at her husband-to-be waiting at the altar. He looked so breathtakingly handsome that part of her still couldn't believe he was marrying *her!* Plain old Emma Lawrence from suburban Maryland. And as if that wasn't enough, he was making her into the countess of Palliser. She laughed every time she thought of it. She—a countess! Oh, if the kids in her old elementary school could see her now!

But then, a lot of them would. Emma looked at her parents, beaming to the point of bursting as they waited to escort her up the aisle. They'd put announcements in every local newspaper from the local pennysaver to the *Washington Post*. "Mr. and Mrs. Ernest A. Lawrence are proud to announce the engagement of their daughter, Emma…" Mother's friends had been green with envy, she'd said.

"Are you ready to go, sweetie?" her father asked, smiling at her with the same pride she used to see when she brought home a good report card. The face was older, the hair a bit grayer, but the twinkle in his eyes was the same as it had always been for her. It warmed her heart.

"We're only about two minutes away now," her mother added, her voice as light as air. She came up behind Emma and laid her hands on her shoulders and turned her around, with a very serious expression on her face. "I have to ask you this, Em. Are you sure you want to do this?"

Emma laughed. "What would you do if I said no?"

"I'd sneak you out the back door and take you home," her mother answered, smoothing the rich bone-colored silk skirt of the designer original wedding gown Lillian had commissioned.

"And never face the bridge club again," her father put in with a wide smile.

Emma patted her mother's arm. "Don't worry, I've never been more sure of anything in my life." She took a deep breath, reveling in the sweet scent of the white roses that lined the aisle to the altar.

Her mother smiled and dabbed a tear away from her eye. "I was sure you were going to say that, but I had to ask."

Emma took her mother's hand and squeezed it. "I'm so lucky to have you. Both of you."

The string quartet began to play the first notes of the wedding march, and Emma took a deep breath. It was time to join Brice at the altar.

Her father held out an arm and Emma slipped her own through it, relaxing against him for a moment before walking past the three hundred guests who were waiting to see her for the first time. Her mother took her place on Emma's other side and they began the long walk up the aisle.

The faces that smiled at her as she passed were like something out of an old movie. Waistcoats, silk, Belgian lace; she wouldn't have been surprised to see a few gold pocket watches on elaborate fobs. It was wonderful. And the smiles were genuine, not patronizing. These people had high regard for Brice, and it didn't matter to them that he was marrying outside of their class. He was happy, and they were glad for him.

As she neared the front of the church, Caroline Fortescue caught Emma's eye and gave a broad smile and a subtle thumbs-up from under her hymnal. Emma couldn't help it, she laughed.

It was the happiest day of her life.

At least, the happiest so far. When she closed her eyes and imagined, she saw a lot of golden moments ahead with Brice. This was only the first.

Before she knew it, the ceremony was over and she was coming back down the aisle, holding her husband's hand in hers. She smiled so much she thought she might tear a facial muscle. Brice looked the same, and he was more relaxed than she could remember seeing him.

"I can't wait to get you alone on that boat," he said. They were taking his family's yacht on a cruise of the Mediterranean as soon as they left the reception.

"We won't be alone," Emma reminded him. "There's the captain and the crew…"

"We'll be alone," he said, with a pirate's smile, leaving no doubt about his intentions. "Lady Palliser, enjoy the daylight now, because I don't intend for either one of us to leave the cabin for several days."

She shushed him, laughing. "People will hear."

"Let them!" he cried, then, in a normal tone, added, "I don't care who knows it, I'm going to ravish my wife." He tightened his hold on her hand. "And I'm going to love her for the rest of my life."

Her face grew warm with a happy flush. "I'll hold you to that."

They stepped out of the church into the sunlight and a blur of faces swam before them, tossing birdseed instead of rice since Emma had heard the rice could choke birds who later came to snack on it.

"Congratulations!" people cried.

"Best wishes!"

Emma's mother and father joined them and hugged them both, with tears in their eyes.

"You take good care of my little girl," her father told Brice, not the least bit intimidated by the younger man's title and position.

Brice gave a respectful bow of the head. "I will, sir."

Her mother dabbed her eyes with a wrinkled handkerchief. "I'm sure he will," she told her husband. "You can see it in the way they look at each other."

All at once, Emma's eyes filled with tears. "Will you two be coming back for Christmas?"

"I've already insisted that they do," Lillian Palliser said, coming up behind Ernest Lawrence. "We'll have an old-fashioned Christmas right here. Helen and I have already begun to plan, haven't we?"

"Yes," Helen Lawrence said, with a wink to Emma. "We're going to stay for three weeks."

Lillian took both of Emma's hands in hers, and moved forward to kiss both cheeks. "Welcome to the family, dear."

"Thank you," Emma said soberly. "I'll do my best to make your son happy."

Lillian and Brice exchanged a look, then the older woman said, with her eyes still on her son, "I believe you will, dear. I believe you will."

Next, a red-haired man who looked vaguely familiar to Emma came up to them. "Well, you did it, old man. I always knew you would." He turned to Emma and smiled. "You should have heard how adoringly he spoke of you before you came. It was enough to give a person cavities."

Brice turned to Emma and answered the query in her eyes. "This," he said, with a sheepish smile, "is John Turnhill."

So *that* was why he looked familiar. She held out her hand to him. "I'm so glad to meet you at last." She gave a sly glance to her husband and said, "I'm a real fan of your work."

"You haven't seen the best of it yet." He stepped aside and gestured to the horse-drawn carriage that waited to take Brice and Emma to the reception. There were cans tied to the back and Just Married scrawled across the back in what appeared to be whipped cream.

John took Emma's hand and helped her into the carriage. "Lady Palliser," he said, bowing deeply.

Brice followed and John bowed again and gave an even more dramatic, "Lord Palliser." He then went to the driver's seat and climbed in.

"Don't tell me you're driving," Brice said, in a bemused tone.

"Can you think of anyone more appropriate?" he asked, raising an eyebrow.

Brice put his arm around Emma. "Maybe not," he said, with a chuckle. "Maybe not."

"After all, it's thanks to me that you two—"

"Let's not go too far," Brice interrupted.

"You may be right." With a shrug, John turned around and slapped the reins down. The horses began a slow trot. John didn't turn around again.

"See that man?" Brice said into Emma's ear as they pulled away from the people. There was a portly man at the edge of the crowd, waving his hat.

"Yes," she said, wondering what Brice was up to now.

"He's a contractor," he said. "He's starting work on adding your laboratory to Sheldale House today."

She caught her breath. "Oh, Brice, really?"

He touched her nose then kissed her on the cheek. "Of course. I know you, Emma, if you spend too much time away from your work you'll go mad. I told him to hire as many people as he needed to, to get it done quickly. It should be finished soon after we get back, in about a month.''

She cupped her hand to his cheek, half-afraid that her pounding heart would burst. ''You're the most thoughtful, wonderful, loving, incredible man in the world, do you know that?''

''I don't know about all that, but you bring out the very best in me.'' He gazed into her eyes for a moment, then captured her mouth in a brief but passionate kiss. ''You've made me the man I always wanted to be.''

Tears came into her eyes. ''He was there all along,'' she said, sniffing lightly.

''But it took you to bring him out,'' Brice said, kissing her again. They rounded a corner and passed the gates of Sheldale House. ''Now he's yours forever.''

''And I'm yours,'' she said, watching as the home they would return to and raise their children in grew smaller and smaller in the distance. ''And we'll live happily ever after.''

* * * * *

Jane Miller gets an unexpected proposal from
her boss in Elizabeth Harbison's
PLAIN JANE MARRIES THE BOSS.
Look for it next month only in
Silhouette Romance.

Coming from Silhouette Romance®:

Cinderella  BRIDES

From rising star

ELIZABETH HARBISON

These women are about to live out their very own fairy tales...but will they live happily ever after?

On sale November 1999
EMMA AND THE EARL (SR #1410)
She thought she'd outgrown dreams of happily-ever-after, yet when American Emma Lawrence found herself a guest of Earl Brice Palliser's lavish estate, he seemed her very own Prince Charming.

On sale December 1999
PLAIN JANE MARRIES THE BOSS (SR #1416)
Sexy millionaire Trey Breckenridge III had finally asked Jane Miller to marry him. She knew he only needed a convenient wife to save his business, so Jane had just three months to show Trey the joys a forever wife could bring!

And look for the fairy tale to continue in January 2000 in
ANNIE AND THE PRINCE.

Cinderella Brides, only from

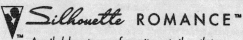

Available at your favorite retail outlet.

If you enjoyed what you just read,
then we've got an offer you can't resist!

Take 2 bestselling love stories FREE!

Plus get a FREE surprise gift!

Clip this page and mail it to Silhouette Reader Service™

IN U.S.A.	**IN CANADA**
3010 Walden Ave.	P.O. Box 609
P.O. Box 1867	Fort Erie, Ontario
Buffalo, N.Y. 14240-1867	L2A 5X3

YES! Please send me 2 free Silhouette Romance® novels and my free surprise gift. Then send me 6 brand-new novels every month, which I will receive months before they're available in stores. In the U.S.A., bill me at the bargain price of $2.90 plus 25¢ delivery per book and applicable sales tax, if any*. In Canada, bill me at the bargain price of $3.25 plus 25¢ delivery per book and applicable taxes**. That's the complete price and a savings of over 10% off the cover prices—what a great deal! I understand that accepting the 2 free books and gift places me under no obligation ever to buy any books. I can always return a shipment and cancel at any time. Even if I never buy another book from Silhouette, the 2 free books and gift are mine to keep forever. So why not take us up on our invitation. You'll be glad you did!

215 SEN CNE7
315 SEN CNE9

Name	(PLEASE PRINT)	
Address	Apt.#	
City	State/Prov.	Zip/Postal Code

* Terms and prices subject to change without notice. Sales tax applicable in N.Y.
** Canadian residents will be charged applicable provincial taxes and GST.
   All orders subject to approval. Offer limited to one per household.
   ® are registered trademarks of Harlequin Enterprises Limited.

SROM99   ©1998 Harlequin Enterprises Limited

Don't miss Silhouette's newest cross-line promotion,

Four royal sisters find their own Prince Charmings as they embark on separate journeys to find their missing brother, the Crown Prince!

The search begins
in October 1999 and
continues through February 2000:

On sale October 1999: **A ROYAL BABY ON THE WAY**
by award-winning author **Susan Mallery** (Special Edition)

On sale November 1999: **UNDERCOVER PRINCESS**
by bestselling author **Suzanne Brockmann** (Intimate Moments)

On sale December 1999: **THE PRINCESS'S WHITE KNIGHT**
by popular author **Carla Cassidy** (Romance)

On sale January 2000: **THE PREGNANT PRINCESS**
by rising star **Anne Marie Winston** (Desire)

On sale February 2000: **MAN...MERCENARY...MONARCH**
by top-notch talent **Joan Elliott Pickart** (Special Edition)

ROYALLY WED
Only in—
SILHOUETTE BOOKS

Available at your favorite retail outlet.

Visit us at www.romance.net

SSERW

**Start celebrating Silhouette's 20th anniversary
with these 4 special titles by
New York Times bestselling authors**

Fire and Rain
by Elizabeth Lowell

King of the Castle
by Heather Graham Pozzessere

State Secrets
by Linda Lael Miller

Paint Me Rainbows
by Fern Michaels

On sale in December 1999

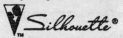

EXTRA! EXTRA!

**The book all your favorite authors
are raving about is finally here!**

**The 1999 Harlequin and Silhouette
coupon book.**

Each page is alive with savings that can't be beat!

**Getting this incredible coupon book is
as easy as 1, 2, 3.**

1. During the months of November and December 1999 buy
   any 2 Harlequin or Silhouette books.

2. Send us your name, address and 2 proofs of purchase (cash
   receipt) to the address below.

3. Harlequin will send you a coupon book worth $10.00 off
   future purchases of Harlequin or Silhouette books in 2000.

Send us 3 cash register receipts as proofs of purchase and
we will send you 2 coupon books worth a total saving of
$20.00 (limit of 2 coupon books per customer).

Saving money has never been this easy.

Please allow 4-6 weeks for delivery. Offer expires December 31, 1999.

I accept your offer! Please send me (a) coupon booklet(s):

Name: _____

Address: _____ City: _____

State/Prov.: _____ Zip/Postal Code: _____

Send your name and address, along with your cash register receipts as
proofs of purchase, to:

In the U.S.: Harlequin Books, P.O. Box 9057, Buffalo, N.Y. 14269
In Canada: Harlequin Books, P.O. Box 622, Fort Erie, Ontario L2A 5X3

Order your books and accept this coupon offer through our web site
http://www.romance.net
Valid in U.S. and Canada only.

PHQ4994R